Weekend Surrender by Lori King

Table of Contents

Dedication
Chapter One
Chapter Two
Chapter Three
Chapter Four
Chapter Five
Chapter Six
Chapter Seven
Chapter Eight
Chapter Nine
Chapter Ten
Chapter Eleven
Chapter Twelve
Chapter Thirteen
Chapter Fourteen
Chapter Fifteen
Chapter Sixteen
Epilogue
Books by Lori King
Excerpt from Rush Against Time
Mated
Rane's Giant

JK Publishing, Inc.

Chapter One

Rachel slammed the closet door behind her as she emerged dressed in her sexiest, country cutie clothes. Her stonewashed blue denim miniskirt barely covered the bottom curves of her ass cheeks. It was paired with a man's red and blue plaid dress shirt, and the shirttails were tied just under her perky B-cup breasts. She left the buttons open so her tits were clearly visible rising out of the top of her blood-red satin pushup bra.

Her tanned midsection was completely bare except for the crystal belly ring that dangled in her belly button. From the back she knew the view would be of the half dollar size daisy tattoo she had gotten when she turned eighteen, just above the top of her black belt. The hand-tooled leather was clasped between her hips bones, with a large belt buckle in the shape of a star. On her feet were a pair of black cowboy boots with silver embellishments, and her long, slim legs were bare.

She was dressed to kill with every intention of causing a few heart attacks tonight. Her chestnut brown hair hung down to the middle of her back in large wavy curls, and she ran her fingers through it carelessly as she walked.

Her makeup was applied with precision so her oversized chocolate brown eyes were nearly as prominent as her blood-red lips. She had always hated the fullness of her lips, but men seemed to love them. Mitch always called them dick sucking lips.

She hated Mitch now.

Mitch deserved Connie Sanders. The bleach blonde tramp had been trying to sink her claws into Mitchell Edwards for more than six months, and she had finally gotten her way. *Well screw them both.* If plastic boobs, and a spray-on tan was what Mitch got off on, then he deserved Connie.

Weekend Surrender
The Surrender Trilogy
Book One

by Lori King

© Copyright September 2013 JK Publishing, Inc.
All cover art and logo © Copyright September 2013 by JK Publishing, Inc.
All rights reserved.

Edited by Caroline Kirby
Artwork by JK Publishing, Inc.
Published by JK Publishing, Inc.

Live Laugh Love!
Lori King

Smashwords Edition, License Notes

This eBook is licensed for your personal enjoyment only. This eBook may not be re-sold or given away to other people. If you would like to share this book with another person, please purchase an additional copy for each recipient. If you are reading this book and did not purchase it or it was not purchased for your use only, then please return to Smashwords.com, and purchase your own copy.

Thank you for respecting the hard work of this author.

This is a work of fiction. Names, places, characters and incidents either are the product of the author's imagination or are used fictitiously and any resemblance to any actual persons, living or dead, organizations, events or locales are entirely coincidental.

No part of this book may be reproduced, stored in a retrieval system, or transmitted by any means without the written permission of the author and publishing company.

Piracy

Please always be aware of where you are purchasing your electronic books and from whom. Only purchase from reputable, licensed individuals such as Amazon, Barnes & Noble, iTunes, etc. If ever in doubt, let the author know of a suspected site illegally selling their works—remember to include a link to the site where you have found a book you suspect of being pirated. It only takes a moment of your time, but you will forever have the gratitude of an author.

About the eBook Purchased

Your purchase of this eBook allows you to only ONE LEGAL copy for your own personal reading on your own personal computer or device. You do not have resale or distribution rights without the prior written permission of both the publisher and the copyright owner of this eBook. This eBook cannot be copied in any format, sold, or otherwise transferred from your computer to another through upload to a file sharing peer-to-peer program, free or for a fee, or as a prize in any contest. Such action is illegal and in violation of the U.S. Copyright Law. Distribution of this eBook, in whole or in part, online, offline, in print or in any way or any other method currently known or yet to be invented, is forbidden. If you do not want this eBook anymore, you must delete it from your computer.

WARNING: The unauthorized reproduction or distribution of this copyrighted work is illegal. Criminal copyright infringement, including infringement without monetary gain, is investigated by the FBI and is punishable by up to 5 years in federal prison and a fine of $250,000.

If you find any e-books being sold or shared illegally, please contact the author or the publishing company.

Email: jkpublishing@jkpublishingbooks.com
JK Publishing bookstore: www.shop.jkpublishingbooks.com

Dedication

I have three groups of people to dedicate this story to. First, I must dedicate it to my Brat Pack. You ladies motivate and support me in ways that you will never understand, and I love you for it. Second, to all of my friends who have encouraged me to make the choices that are right for me, even if it goes against the grain. You know who you are, and I want you to know that I appreciate you. And last but certainly not least, this is for my husband and children who keep me grounded while pushing me to reach for the stars. I love you four more than you can ever know. As always I hope to Live, Laugh, and Love like today is my only chance.
    -Lori

Rachel was going to go out and find a man to fuck her heartbreak away. She wanted raw, dirty, raunchy sex. Not the soft, gentle missionary sex Mitch seemed to favor. She wanted to be shoved against a wall, or held down by her wrists as a large muscular man devoured her completely. That's why she created this plan.

It was a Friday night, and that meant a packed house at Robin's, the local bar that Rachel had waited tables at through college. She had met Mitch there, and he would no doubt be there tonight playing darts with his cronies, while Connie giggled and preened over a watered down margarita. So in order to prove to the world that Rachel Lia Morgan was completely and utterly over her ex-boyfriend, she was going on the prowl on his turf.

There were usually dozens of hot men at Robin's on the weekends. All of the local ranchers and ranch hands from the outskirts of Stone River usually hit the bar on Friday night looking for some action. Never before had Rachel considered indulging in a one-night stand, but tonight was her night.

She spritzed a little bit of her favorite perfume on her throat, and then grabbed her small purse. On her way out the door she noticed her cell phone was blinking with a missed message. She climbed into her silver Ford F150 as she hit the play message button.

"Rach, I know you don't want to talk to me, but I want to apologize. I didn't mean for you to find out about Connie like that…Rach? Please call me so we can talk this out. You can't just throw two years out the window. I made a mistake, damn it—"

The voice clicked off as she hit the delete button, and dropped her phone back into her purse. Mitch could beg and plead all he wanted, but she had already made her peace with their breakup. She wasn't interested in his excuses anymore. She turned the volume up on her truck radio, so Miranda Lambert's tune "Mama's Broken Heart" blared out the windows into the night, and headed toward her freedom.

The bar's parking lot was packed with work trucks. With exception of only a handful of cars that probably belonged to the female patrons of the bar. Rachel backed her truck into a small parking stall at the back edge of the lot, right next to a black Dodge Ram Quad Cab that looked like it had rolled off the lot and onto the ranch just a few hours ago. Realizing she had parked rather close to the truck, she carefully opened her door, and slipped out into the small space.

A large masculine hand covered hers, where it rested on the top edge of her truck door, and she gasped.

"Sunshine, if you nick my new truck with your door, I'm going to have to spank that cute little ass raw." The voice in her ear sent a shiver over her skin, and she flushed at his words.

She turned her head to see who was behind her that would have any right to speak to her like that, and she nearly groaned out loud when her brown eyes met those of Parker Brooks. Parker Brooks was one of the four Brooks brothers who owned Brooks Pastures-a local cattle ranch. The four brothers shared two things in common, their love of ranching, and their smoking hot good looks. Dark hair, dark eyes, long lean muscular cowboy bodies, all tucked up under a cowboy hat. It made Rachel's blood sing just thinking about the four of them.

Holding her breath she dropped her gaze from his dark eyes down to his sexy mouth, and she felt her own tongue dart out to wet her lips unconsciously. His raised eyebrow told her that he noticed, and she shook her head slightly to clear her lust fogged brain.

"I'm sorry, Parker. I did park a little close there, but no worries, I was careful," she said with a smile she hoped would distract him from the increase in her breathing, and the rise and fall of her breasts.

It clearly didn't work, because his eyes shifted from her lips directly down the front of her shirt, and then they dragged lower. His gaze drifted from her golden colored abs, down to her booted feet, and then he reached out and tugged her hand free of the truck door. Surprised, she followed his lead when he turned her around so her back was to him again. A long, low whistle had goose bumps forming on her arms, but the finger stroking over her tattoo in the small of her back was what had her creaming her panties.

"Holy shit, sunshine. Who let you out of the house dressed like that?" he asked in a gravelly rough voice that nearly knocked Rachel's knees out from underneath her.

The meaning of his question sunk in, and her irritation overcame her libido. "Last I looked in the mirror I was a grown woman, cowboy. I don't need anyone's permission or approval of my wardrobe."

Parker let her go when she tugged her hand out of his. She slammed her truck door and started to move out from between the two vehicles. "You might be grown up, but wearing a skirt like that is asking for trouble."

She paused and looked back over her shoulder. "Maybe that's exactly what I wanted," she said with a shrug of her shoulders.

His slow, sexy smile made her mouth go dry, and she swallowed hard. "If you want trouble, little girl, all you need to do is ask."

Trying to cover up her nerves at his deliberately seductive invitation, she snorted out a laugh, "If I decide I want your kind of trouble, I won't need to ask." Tossing her hair back over her shoulder, she headed for the door of the bar.

Before she could pull it open, a large hand reached around her for the door handle, and another equally large hand settled on her hip. Whipping her head violently, ready to give Parker Brooks a piece of her mind, she froze in place when it was his brother, Hudson's face only inches from hers.

"Hey, honey," he said with a quick smile, and a wink, "Let me get the door for you."

"Thanks, Hudson," she responded, sighing with relief that that was all he said. She wanted a wild fling, but the Brooks brothers were out of her league for multiple reasons.

They were all at least ten years older than her twenty-four years, and they were all wickedly sexy men. The rumors around town were the four brothers shared their women, and right at this moment, looking into Hudson's heated cocoa-colored gaze, she would have believed it. She had an inkling he had heard her interaction with Parker, but she wasn't going to tempt fate by asking.

Instead she tipped her chin up and turned back to the door, only to realize that it wasn't Hudson's hand on her. Sawyer Brooks stood on her other side with his hand resting lightly on the curve of her hip, and the rest of his body leaning nonchalantly against the door jam.

"Rachel," he said softly, and her pulse took off racing. Okay, the idea of having a sexy one-night stand had merit, but now that she was surrounded by large muscular men, she wasn't so sure she could go through with the reality. "No need to rush off. How are you tonight?"

Blinking in surprise, she answered automatically in a snotty tone, "I'm fan-fuckin-tastic, Sawyer, thank you for asking."

His eyes darkened with irritation, and his lip curled up in a grimace. "Don't use language like that, you're a lady, and ladies shouldn't curse."

Rachel couldn't help it. She burst into a roar of laughter. Not giggles, or chuckles, but large loud belly laughs. "Are you kidding me? Sawyer Brooks, I have seen you compete in the local rodeo, and heard the nastiness that spews from those luscious lips. Do you really think you can tell *me* not to curse?"

Sawyer focused in on the one phrase from her whole little speech that he liked, "Luscious lips, huh?" Those sexy lips curved up into an equally sinful smile that had her pussy tightening, and her thighs clenching.

She forced herself to roll her eyes, even as a blush covered her cheeks. "Whatever. I'm going inside to get a drink, dance a little, and maybe play some pool. Excuse me, gentlemen." She reached again for the door handle, only to have a new set of hands settle on her shoulders and tug her backwards until she stumbled. Instead of falling on her ass though, her plump butt cheeks settled against the rough denim of a man's Levi's, and a heavy arm banded under her ribs holding her upright.

"Apologize, Rachel, you were rude to Sawyer, and he was just trying to teach you a few manners," Parker's voice rumbled against her ear, and she bit her tongue hard to swallow her moan of lust.

"No. Let me go, Parker, this isn't funny," she ground out, and she began to struggle to get out of Parker's strong grip.

"Stop it. You'll end up hurting yourself. Now, Sawyer and Hudson deserve a sincere apology, and then I want an explanation as to what you're doing at Robin's dressed like a two bit hooker on fight night?" Ice coated his words, and she stilled in his arms. A wave of hurt and embarrassment went through her. Did she really look so bad? She had put on the clothes that made her feel the sexiest.

"I apologize if I've offended anyone, but I have plans inside the bar that include a bottle of tequila, and a few spins around the dance floor. You are currently delaying my plans. I have no intention of prostituting myself, because I've never in my life felt the need to ask a man for sex. I'm dressed in clothing I picked out, and like. I don't personally give a damn if you approve or not, Mr. Brooks." She focused all of her anger on her words, and when he finally released her she sighed heavily, "Thank you. Have a lovely evening, gentlemen."

Hudson tugged the door open, and Sawyer stepped back from the doorway allowing her to saunter past him. Once she was safely in the bar, she let out a heavy, shaky breath and made her way across the room directly into the bathroom to settle her nerves. It might take more than a drink or two to wipe the Brooks brothers from her fantasies tonight.

Chapter Two

"What the hell is she doing *here* dressed like *that*?" Rogan Brooks asked his brothers. Unbeknownst to Rachel, he was standing in the shadows of the building watching the whole scene. Rachel Morgan was just about the hottest piece of ass to ever walked through Stone River, Texas, and the Brooks brothers were only red-blooded men. They had fantasized along with the rest of the male population about getting the wild little filly saddle broke, but not one of them had ever made a move or laid a hand on her until tonight.

Of course she hadn't been single for the last few years either. She had been with that disgusting piece of cow shit, Mitch Edwards. He was the mayor's son, and the local playboy wannabe. Now that she was single, she was apparently ready to get back into the dating scene, and after years of fantasizing and dreaming about her, the four Brooks brothers finally had their chance. The little girl they had known her whole life had grown up to be a stunning, intelligent woman with a sparkle that outshined everyone around her. Rogan hadn't wanted a serious relationship with a woman other than Rachel since the night she'd turned twenty-one.

She probably didn't even remember the events of the night, but after she toasted her birthday a few too many times, Rogan had been the one to drive her and her best friend, Zoey, home. He would never forget the weight of her in his arms and against his chest as he carried her from the car to the house, and left her on the sofa in her mother's care. At first he had scolded himself, feeling guilty that he was having dirty thoughts about a woman so much younger than he was, but as she grew older and came into her own, he realized her age didn't matter. Rachel was who he wanted. He just hadn't quite figured out how to tell her yet.

"I don't know, but she is definitely looking for trouble tonight. Did you see how her cheeks got real pink when

Parker grabbed her? I think she likes a little bit of rough play," Hudson said with a groan and a chuckle.

"What's next?" Rogan asked impatiently. "I know we said we were going to give her some time, but damn it, I don't want her to go fucking some random guy."

That sobered his brothers, and soothed his frustration. They were all in agreement. She was the perfect woman to handle the four Brooks brothers. Since they were teenagers, they had been sharing women amongst them for sex. Sometimes one woman for every two brothers, and occasionally one for all four of them, but never one to keep. Now they had a chance, and it looked like it was about to be washed away with a bottle of Tequila.

"Let's go. If she wants to drink, dance, and play pool, she's going to have more company than she ever imagined. And if she wants to go home with someone, it will be us," Parker said, and the other three brothers nodded in agreement.

They headed into the bar, and Rogan's eyes scanned the room looking for a waterfall of brown curls on top of a delicious curvy body. Sawyer spotted her first, leaning against the bar chatting with a local ranch hand. She had her arms crossed under her small breasts pushing them up and out, much to Rogan's dismay and delight. She was in full throttle flirt mode, and he wanted to shut it down immediately.

Walking across the bar as a unit they surrounded her, with Hudson slipping in between her and the drooling cowboy she had been chatting with, and Parker and Sawyer on her right.

"Hey!" she yelped in surprise as Rogan's arms went around her waist, and he pulled her back up against his chest. The bare skin of her belly was soft and warm, and he knew he would never forget that moment. She felt so perfect in his arms, and her fresh scent flooded his brain.

"Hey there, sexy. I hear you said hi to my brothers but didn't stick around to say hello to me. I'm hurt," he said with a playful pout, and she rolled her eyes giggling.

"Is that the story they told? I don't quite remember it that way. I seem to recall Parker threatening me, then Hudson delaying me from my plans, Sawyer bossing me around, and finally Parker playing daddy, and manhandling me," she said with a sigh, but he nearly groaned out loud when she settled more firmly into him instead of pulling away.

"I haven't even started manhandling you yet, sunshine. Although I would be happy to play with you anytime, but I prefer to be called Parker over daddy," Parker said, and her eyes grew wide. She stared into the mirror over the bar at the four men surrounding her.

Rogan wondered what was going through her pretty little head when her eyes glazed over slightly, and her heart rate increased. She shook her head as though to clear her thoughts and frowned.

"Guys, you're seriously cramping my style. No man is going to want to get close to me with all four of you hanging around," she said in a pleading tone.

"Good," Sawyer muttered under his breath, and Rogan grinned.

"That's the idea," Hudson said, and Rachel's eyes nearly bugged out of her head.

"Huh?"

"Rachel, we get it. You just broke up with Mitch, and you're trying to prove something. To yourself, or to him, it doesn't matter. What does matter is that we don't want you playing the field. We want you to come home with us," Rogan said, bending to kiss the top of her head lightly. She stared into his mirror image in shock, but her body was pulsing in his arms. Whether she admitted it or not, she wanted them.

"Come on, stop playing around, guys," she said with a toss of her hair.

Silence reigned for a few heartbeats, and then Parker slid his hand up her arm until he was gripping her chin between his thumb and forefinger forcing her to look him in the eyes. "Rachel, think about it. Four men who want to please you, and give you more orgasms than you can imagine."

She snorted in disbelief still staring into Parker's eyes. "Would you stop teasing me? It's really rather rude."

Rogan could see Parker's jaw clench in frustration. Parker hated being denied. Rachel was going to learn the hard way about his Alpha male nature if she kept it up. He knew he had to interfere before the two of them began spitting fire at each other.

"So what exactly is your plan for the evening, Rach?" Rogan said softly, regaining her attention.

She blinked, and her tongue darted out to lick her full lips. Rogan wanted to capture those lips with his own, and worship them with his tongue. He wondered if she had any idea how many fantasies she had created in his brain with that quick little unconscious gesture. Her almost bare back was still pressed against his abdomen, and he knew she could feel his erection through his jeans. Just to tease her, he lightly grazed his thumb over the delicate jewel hanging from her navel. Her sharp intake of breath told him he was successful.

"I'm going to finish my drink, and then I suppose I'm going to ask some lonely cowboy to dance with me," she said, gripping her glass tighter in her hands. She didn't push him away from her, so Rogan continued to trace his finger over the petal soft skin of her belly.

"You have four lonely cowboys right here, ask away," Sawyer said with a grin.

She shook her head slightly, and blinked rapidly. "What is going on? You guys have barely spoken to me for nearly a year, and all of a sudden you want me to participate in some sort of raunchy gang bang?"

"You weren't exactly on the market, honey, but now that you cut that douche bag Mitch loose, you're fair game," Hudson said softly, and Rogan could see his brother's hand stroking up and down Rachel's exposed thigh. A shiver went through her body, and her breathing sped up.

"Fair game? So now I'm a prize. Like a stuffed animal at the carnival? Really, guys this isn't funny." Her gorgeous brown eyes were snapping with irritation now, and her cheeks were flushed pink. Rogan had to steel his own nerves not to flip her over his lap for thinking so lowly of herself.

"Rach, you're a prize alright, but I wouldn't compare you to stuffed animal. More like a gold medal for an athlete. Of course, I would prefer to not have to compete, but if you need to dance, then let's dance," he said, as he spun her bar stool around so she was facing him, and pulled her up off the seat.

He didn't give her time to argue or agree. He just pulled her along with him toward the dance floor. The sound of Toby Keith's husky baritone voice filled Rogan's ears, as he pulled her compact little body against his big frame. Her head fit perfectly under his chin, and her pert breasts pressed tightly against his ribs. He let his hands settle on the curve of her lower back, and the rise of her ass, and he began to sway the two of them to the music.

After several moments Rachel tipped her head to look up at him warily. Doing so gave him an unimpeded view straight down the open collar of her shirt, and into her cleavage. His cock thickened in his jeans, and his mouth grew wet thinking about licking his way down to that sensitive crevice.

"Rogan? I'm not sure what's going on, but I don't need babysitters. I'm a big girl, and I came here tonight to have a good time. I don't want anyone feeling obligated to take care of me," she said with a determined tilt to her sharp little chin.

Rogan chuckled, and dropped a quick kiss on her upturned lips, drawing a startled gasp from her. "Rachel, obligated is the *last* thing I feel toward you right now. I can guess what you came here to do, and I'm offering our services. If you look to your left you'll see my brothers watching us closely, waiting for their turn to hold you tonight. That should be enough to prove we aren't playing with you."

She turned her head, and her mouth dropped open in surprise. Rogan thought for a moment that she even stopped breathing, until she turned confused eyes back to him, and he realized they were shimmering with tears.

"I don't like being the butt of the joke," she whispered, and he growled low in his throat in exasperation.

"Damn it, woman, we're not fucking playing with you," he snapped, and she stepped backwards instinctively moving away from his angry words. He gripped her wrists, and pulled her along with him until they stood before his three brothers, who looked at him questioningly. "She doesn't believe we actually want her. She thinks we're playing a joke on her."

"Fuck that!"

"Are you kidding me?"

"Shit."

****

Rachel could feel the hot blush that stole up her cheeks and down her throat to her chest. Her heart skipped a beat as they all turned glares of disbelief on her. She couldn't seem to catch her breath, and she could feel her body becoming hot and tingly surrounded by their four muscular bodies.

"I just don't get it, why now?" she finally managed to choke out.

"We told you, you broke up with Mitch," Hudson said, with a shrug of his shoulders. "We may have a reputation, but we aren't home wreckers. You and Mitchy-boy were pretty tight for a while, and we weren't trying to ruin your life."

"So if I had been single earlier—" she was trying hard to wrap her brain around it. This was the Brooks brothers. The four hottest men in town, and they were asking her to have a group sex orgy with them. It was beyond comprehension.

Rogan interrupted her musings, "We agreed to give you some time to get over your break up, but then you showed up at the bar looking hot as sin, and twice as dangerous, and…shit…woman you're giving half the men at the bar wet dreams to last them the next decade."

"Why are you out here displaying your body for strangers, Rachel?" Parker asked. Of the four of them, he intimidated her the most. There was something about his cool controlled demeanor that exuded power, and made her want to drop to her knees at his feet and beg him to touch her. Honestly, with Hudson on her left, Rogan behind her, Parker on her right, and Sawyer in front of her, she was in the perfect position to drop to her knees. The dirty thought rang in her brain making her pussy clench.

"Because I was hoping a stranger might bite," she answered with the automatic bratty tone she knew got under Parker's skin.

"Oh, I promise you I'll bite, baby," Sawyer said with a playful grin, and before she could react, he bent down and took her ear lobe between his teeth biting gently.

She moaned and her knees buckled at the erotic sensation. Sawyers arms wrapped around her, holding her up and cupping her ass at the same time he pressed a gentle kiss to her neck just below her ear.

"Shit, baby, if you react like that when it's just your ear in my mouth, I wonder how you'll react when I bite your pretty little nipples," he murmured, and white hot fire shot through Rachel's body straight to her clit.

Her hands came up to rest against his chest, and she tipped her head back to look up at him with slightly blurry vision. "They're very sensitive," she whispered, and then instantly realized she had spoken out loud, when three identical groans sounded from around her. Sawyer's sensuous lips spread into a wide smile.

"Good, I can't wait to taste them," he responded, his words making her tremble in his arms.

"Come home with us, Rachel," Rogan said from just over her shoulder, and she turned her wide eyes in his direction.

She stared into his dark brown eyes, not exactly sure what she was looking for but knowing this decision was going to alter her life monumentally.

"Let us take you home, and make you ours," Sawyer said, running his hands in sexy circles over her ass cheeks. He pressed her tighter to his body, and she could feel the bulge under his zipper against her belly. His words were a heavy weight in her brain though, and she froze.

"For tonight?" she asked, and she waited as the four men had a silent exchange between them.

"Trust us. Give us at least the weekend, Rachel," Hudson said softly, and she felt her heart jump again.

"You guys are crazy," she said quietly, hearing the doubt and fear in her own voice.

"Yep, probably but, sexy lady, we aren't joking," Rogan said, moved up against her back. Sawyer pulled his arms back and Rogan's hands came around her middle until his thumbs were stroking over the soft undersides of her breasts. She moaned while he ground his hard cock against the small of her back.

"And what if I decline?" She turned her head to the side so she could see Parker close the gap between them. She could feel Hudson's body against her other side, and her brain grew fuzzy from their proximity. Being surrounded by all four of them, in the middle of the town's hottest bar, was *not* how she had envisioned tonight going, but she couldn't deny her physical response to them. Her eyes were fastened on Parker's as he reached up to grip her chin in his hand.

"Then we walk away, and you go back to playing bar tease," Parker said, letting his anger harden his tone.

"I didn't say I was declining, but a girl's got to know all of her choices. What exactly happens at the end of the weekend?" she asked with a small smile at his upset.

"You get to decide that on Sunday. Hopefully you will have fallen madly in love with all of us, and want to stay at the ranch forever," Hudson said playfully, and Rachel jerked her head around to glare at him. How could he joke about love and forever? That was ridiculous. It was just sex, and that was all it would ever be.

"Cut that shit out. I may be young, but I'm not stupid. Here's the deal, I won't lie and say I'm not intrigued by your offer, but I don't want false promises. If you want sex, I can do sex. Hell, I can't even pretend I don't want to have sex with you," she paused, swallowing hard, "I will willingly spend the weekend with you—with all of you—on one condition." She met Sawyer's hot gaze as she tipped her head back. The back of her head rested against Rogan's hard chest, and she could feel his breath on her temple.

"Name it."

"Sunday night we all walk away friends. No harm no foul. We act as if nothing ever happened, and no one gets hurt. Sex is all I want right now guys. I'm not in the market for more, and no matter what you might say right now, you don't want more," she said with a small shake of her head. She felt apprehensive, but determined.

Chapter Three

Rogan's heart nearly stopped in his chest. She was agreeing to spend the weekend with them. Finally, after several years of masturbating to his fantasies of her, he was going to not only get her in his bed, but he was going to get to share her with his brothers. His cock throbbed at the mental images flooding his brain. Tamping down his lust, he listened to the rest of her speech. He could hear the nerves in her tone, as she laid out her conditions. He hated that she would doubt their desire for her, or put limitations on the possibility of a relationship, but Rogan had never admired her more. She was a spitfire, and she would give them hell, but damn it was going to be fun convincing her that she was wrong.

Parker looked up meeting Rogan's gaze, and nodded. Hudson and Sawyer both grunted in agreement, and then Rachel nodded her acceptance. Rogan couldn't help it, a huge grin burst over his face, and he spun her around into his arms. Before she could react, he pressed tightly against her smaller frame and took her mouth in a desperately hot kiss. Hopefully by Sunday night, she would understand their desire for her wasn't in a one night stand, but in a lifetime.

Breaking off the kiss, he turned and started dragging her to the door, uncaring that multiple people stopped to stare at them. He knew one of his brothers would pay her tab, and all he could think about right now was getting her out of this bar, and out of town. He wasn't willing to give her time to back out of this, he wanted to sink into her hot pussy as quickly as possible, and that meant getting her naked.

Reaching their trucks, he turned back to her. "Give me your keys," he said more harshly than he had intended and she paled a little. Freezing he brought her hands up to his lips and kissed her knuckles while he met her wary eyes, "I'm sorry, sexy, but I don't want to take the chance on you changing your mind. I just figured I would drive you and your truck back to your place, so you can grab a change of clothes…then again you probably won't be needing many clothes between now and Sunday night."

"You aren't driving my baby," she said with a shake of her head, and a laugh. "I don't let anyone drive my truck."

"Fine, you drive, but I'm going with you," he said with a sigh of relief. There was no way he would pursue an argument right now. He wasn't going to take a chance on her backing out.

The moment she turned on the truck, the sounds of Chris Young singing "Getting You Home" overwhelmed the closed cab around them.

The words fit Rogan's thoughts at the moment, and he smirked at her. The pink blush on her cheeks told him she was thinking the same thing. A ripple of pleasure went through his body, and he settled back into the seat with a grin on his face. The ride to Rachel's place was quick. Her body language told him that she was nervous, but she continued to amaze him by pushing aside her reservations. She sighed with relief when they pulled into her driveway.

Rogan grinned at the image of Rachel's tiny figure in the driver's seat of her big silver pickup. She drove it like she did everything, with single-minded stubbornness, and with her whole heart and soul. Secretly he hoped she would apply the same vigor to a relationship with the four of them, but for now all he was promised was a weekend of wickedly sinful sex, and his cock throbbed for it.

His brothers had followed them to Rachel's place, and quickly met them as they were getting out of the truck. Parker walked her to the door while the other three followed along. Rogan almost laughed out loud at the irritation gracing her beautiful visage when Parker took her key from her hand and unlocked her door.

"I'm a big girl, Parker—" she snapped, but the words broke off when Parker grabbed her by the back of the neck and tugged her face closer to his.

"I'm not doing it for you because I don't think you can handle it, sunshine. I want to take care of you. You deserve to be treated like a beautiful woman should be," he said firmly in a deeper more demanding tone. Rogan had to bite his tongue not to laugh out loud as Rachel's jaw went slack, and her eyes glazed over.

Parker kissed her mouth, and Rogan could see his tongue dart out to run over her pretty pink lips, before he pulled away, and physically turned her toward the interior of the house. She jumped when Parker lightly slapped her ass, and her frown said it all. Seeming to think better of starting a fight, she turned and took off down the hallway.

Assuming she was going to her room to put together an overnight bag, Rogan wandered through her small home freely. She had no family pictures on the walls, but she had a few knickknacks including a small collection of teddy bear figurines on a shelf over the television. Next to the sofa was a table with a lamp and an e-reader on it. Without even thinking about it, Rogan picked up the small tablet and flipped it on. He scanned through her reading selections, and his mouth fell open. Ms. Rachel Morgan was a dirty, kinky freak.

"Hudson, look!" he whispered loudly, and showed Hudson what he had found.

"Shit!" Hudson said in a tight voice, and he passed the e-reader on to Sawyer, whose face flushed slightly when he read the entries.

"What are you crazy shits doing?" Parker snapped as he came back into the living room. Sawyer handed it to him, and Parker's mouth dropped open. "Well, well, well. Rachel isn't quite the innocent we suspected."

A gasp from the hallway had them all turning to face a furious and embarrassed woman. "What the hell are you doing? Why are you snooping through my things?" She stomped over, and snatched the e-reader from Parker's hands holding it behind her defensively.

"So you have some fantasies, what's the big deal, sunshine? We're planning on making those fantasies real within the next hour," Parker said, and Rogan smiled widely at her blush.

"It's private. I don't share that with anyone," she said, looking a little bit hurt. Rogan stepped forward, but he wasn't fast enough. Sawyer pulled her into his arms, and when her mouth fell open in shock, he took advantage of it, kissing her until she was breathless and panting.

"There is no reason to keep your fantasies and desires a secret. They are part of you, baby, and we want every bit of you. If you hold back, I have a feeling Parker will jump at the chance to spank you," Sawyer said with a low chuckle, and her nervous eyes darted back over her shoulder at Parker who quirked his eyebrow at her. Rogan could see her swallow hard again, and he laughed out loud.

"Chill out, Parker, you're scaring her. Rach, if you have any fantasies you want fulfilled, you have four men at your beck and call. Now, did you get what you needed? I want to get you home." At her nod, Rogan picked up the backpack she had left on the hallway floor, and went to the front door. Sawyer led her out followed by Parker, and then Hudson.

Rogan reached around and made sure the front door was locked before joining his brothers and their woman at the truck. There was no doubt in his mind, after spending the weekend with the Brooks brothers, she would be theirs—body and soul.

****

Rachel's body was trembling with need, and they hadn't even started touching her. She was being pressed tightly between Sawyer and Parker in the front seat of Parker's truck for the twenty minute drive to their ranch. The cab was comfortably large for normal sized people, but with the oversized muscular bodies of the Brooks brothers, it felt slightly claustrophobic.

"I heard you got the sale on the Martin's ranch," Rogan said from the back seat.

Twisting to answer him, she nodded, "Yeah, just booked it on Tuesday. That's my biggest sale to date."

"Congratulations! That ranch is prime grazing land. Who bought it?" Parker said.

"Tanner Kegan did," she answered, and then giggled when all four brothers cursed. The Kegan ranch was the only other ranch around with a reputation to match Brooks

Pastures. Adding more property to their already extensive ranch was a huge boon for the Kegan family.

"Should have seen that coming," Rogan said under his breath, "Kegan has been talking about expanding for a couple of years now."

"I have it on good authority the Rafts are considering putting their place up for sale next month," she said slyly, feeling pleased to be sharing a piece of knowledge that might help the brothers build their ranch. Her real estate career was really the only thing she had lately to focus on. Her mother had moved to Oklahoma City recently to take a new job leaving her here alone, and she had never had a relationship with her slug of a father, so being the area's top realtor meant a great deal to her. It gave her purpose.

"No shit?" Hudson asked excitedly. "That place is nearly three hundred acres!"

"Three hundred acres that border our property. So why are they selling, Rach?" Rogan asked.

"It's kind of sad actually. Diana Raft found out she has breast cancer. Randal said he wants to retire and spend what time she has left focused on her." Emotion made her voice crack, and Sawyer's arm tightened around her shoulders while Parker reached out and squeezed her thigh in support.

"I can understand that. I think those two have been married as long as I've been alive," Rogan said from the backseat.

"Thirty-nine years this August," she responded, resting her head on Sawyer's shoulder comfortably.

"*Longer* than I've been alive!" Rogan said in a soft voice.

"He loves her so much. They are both really torn up about the diagnosis." She fought to keep her emotions in check. She was an easy crier, and the last thing she wanted was to fall apart in front of the four brothers.

To their credit, they kept the rest of the conversation light and relaxed as they tossed jokes and insults back and forth between each other, and even teased her some about her choice in ex-boyfriends. They asked intelligent questions about her job, and about mutual friends, keeping her included in their conversation at all times. She wasn't sure if they were trying to put her at ease, or get to know her, but she embraced it and answered them honestly.

She had always had a weakness for the four of them, but then again what woman in Stone River hadn't? That was the problem, she had to protect her emotions and keep a distance between it and them in order for this to work. If she let them, they would steal her heart and then, she would be crushed when she had to walk away on Sunday. It wasn't fair, but that was the deal.

As they attentively helped her from the truck and led her up to their front door, she wondered if she had completely lost her mind when she accepted their invitation. Was she really capable of handling four men at once? Especially Parker…he was so intense, and bossy. Could she really do this? She let them lead her into the ranch house, and she didn't even argue when they didn't let her carry her bag or her purse. She just went willingly, trying to calm the steady rumble of butterflies in her belly.

Hudson wrapped one arm around her shoulders and led her through the first floor of the ranch house on a tour. Their home was large, and beautiful, but it definitely bespoke bachelors, and needed a woman's touch. The only main room that wasn't cluttered was the kitchen, which was relatively spotless.

"Do you guys cook?" Rachel asked as she sat at the kitchen table.

"I'm the cook in the house. These guys would burn water if I let them near a stove," Sawyer said playfully as he turned the fire on under a saucepot. "Do you like Italian?"

She nodded, and returned his smile. He seemed pleased, and went to work creating some sort of red sauce in the pan in front of him. Before she could say anymore he was giving out instructions. "Ro, grab some spaghetti noodles and get them on the stove. Parker, you should probably check in with Mack before we lock up for the night, and Hudson, get the lady a drink would you?" Sawyer moved around the room gracefully handling the food preparation and leaving her speechless.

"Who is Mack?" Rachel asked.

"Our main ranch hand. He lives in a cabin on the East edge of the ranch, and he is the only one that lives on the property. He watches the place when we're not around," Sawyer answered without a pause.

Parker hesitated for a moment as though irritated to be given his marching orders, before he nodded his agreement and left out the side door to speak to whoever Mack was. Rachel grew nervous as she watched them all working efficiently while she sat like a lump on a log letting them coddle her. Hudson put a glass of white wine in front of her, and pressed a quick kiss to her forehead before he moved on to another task leaving her blushing and flustered. After a few more moments, she decided any task was better than no task.

"Can I help with anything?" her offer was rewarded with a million dollar smile from Sawyer.

"Do you cook?" he asked, tilting his head to look her over.

"What country girl in this region doesn't cook?" she threw back arrogantly, and he laughed.

"Good, you're on bread. It will be nice to have someone around who knows butter from bananas. There's a loaf of French bread in the bread box, and I'm sure there's garlic in the fridge." He waited for her nod of acceptance before he turned back to the sauce he was preparing. She couldn't resist running her eyes over his body while he wasn't looking. How was it possible for a man to make a pair of Wranglers look that damn good?

Rachel focused on the task she had been given, and listened as they all bantered back and forth. You would think they were having a regular evening meal, not preparing a feast before they screwed her brains out. Images of the four men stripping her clothing off, and having their wicked way with her, had her blood pumping hard in her ears, and she nearly forgot about the male bodies surrounding her in the ranch kitchen. She jumped and a squeak slipped from her throat when Rogan moved behind her, and stroked his hand down the split of her ass.

"Hey!" she yelped, nailing him with an annoyed glare, as she waved a bread knife at him. He lifted both hands and smiled innocently.

"Sorry, close quarters, sexy," he said with a wink, and she felt her anger dissipate.

"Mmm hmm. I'll just bet. You shouldn't play grab ass when I'm holding a knife. I could accidentally slip and eliminate appendages," she joked.

"Nah, I'm not worried. You haven't gotten any use out of it yet, there isn't a chance in hell you're going to damage it," Rogan teased back, and he winked at her flushed cheeks.

A moment later it was Hudson who was grabbing a handful of her ass as she moved past him to the refrigerator. This time the only acknowledgement from her was a gasp. She refused to give him the satisfaction of facing him, so instead she continued what she was doing—bending to grab the butter from the bottom shelf of the fridge.

A hard erection pressed against the crack of her ass, causing her stomach to drop to her feet, and her throat to nearly close completely. This time she couldn't keep her groan of desire inside, and Parker groaned back.

"Has anyone ever told you that you have a spectacular ass, sunshine?" he asked as she stood up in front of him, and he rubbed his cock along the seam of her cheeks.

She shook her head, and then let it fall back onto his shoulder. His hands clenched at her denim covered hips tightly, and he pressed a kiss just under her ear, drawing a whimper from her chest. Goose bumps spread out over her skin, and her nipples sharpened into hard points.

Someone relieved her of the butter still in her hands, so Parker could turn her in his arms. Pressing his muscular body tightly against her front, he swooped in for a kiss, and she reacted wantonly. Her hands slid up to grip his short, dark hair at the nape of his neck, and she arched her breasts into his hard body. His tongue battled with hers for possession of the kiss, and when she finally melted and opened to him, she could feel his pleasure at her submission, like sinful strokes over her skin.

When he released her mouth she was trembling, and her breath came out in choppy pants. The masculine self-satisfied smirk on his face didn't even irritate her. Instead she found a part of her wanted to continue to make him happy.

Lifting his head, he stared down into her eyes, and whispered, "Sweet." And her heart thudded in her chest as he released her and spun her around until she was facing Hudson who leaned against the fridge with a grin on his face, and the butter in his hands.

"I love how you look with pink cheeks, honey," Hudson said, and he leaned forward stopping just centimeters from her lips. Her mouth dropped open in preparation for a kiss, only to be frozen when he did nothing but slide his tongue along her bottom lip. "And I love how you taste."

He pressed the butter into her trembling hands, turned her back toward the kitchen counter, and nudged her forward. She moved automatically and silently back to the bread she had been working on. Her mind was fuzzy, and she couldn't seem to put two thoughts together as she coated the French bread in garlicky butter.

She was able to watch the four men as they moved around the kitchen laughing and joking with each other for several minutes before she had to ask the question plaguing her mind.

"Why me?" she said softly, and when they all grew quiet but didn't speak, she asked it louder. "Why me? Every woman in town wants you and with just a crook of your little finger, she would gratefully drop to her knees for the four of you. So what makes me so special?"

Rogan was the closest to her, so he was the first to reach her. Gripping her chin, he tipped her head back so she was forced to meet his eyes. She was surprised to see the emotion that filled his gaze, but she quickly dismissed it as a trick of the light. No way they actually felt anything for her, this was just sex. She had to keep reminding herself this was just a weekend fling to cut loose, and give her her confidence back.

"Rachel, you don't seem to understand that *you* are the one we want. We don't want the other women. I think I speak for all of us, but I will tell you what I personally want. I want a sexy brunette, with legs up to her ears, and the hottest navel piercing I've ever seen. I want the spicy woman with a sharp tongue, that melts when I kiss her, and isn't afraid to put me in my place when I'm being an ass. I want your body, and your heart, and I want to keep them." With every word his brown eyes darkened, and Rachel knew her own eyes widened. Her heart was racing in her chest, and her knees were shaking again.

"You can't keep me," she whispered shakily.

"Why not?" he asked with a raised eyebrow.

"Rogan, you don't have to give me sweet words to get me into your bed. I'll go willingly, but I don't want you guys to play with my emotions. This is supposed to be fun. I just wanted to know why you singled me out tonight?" she said, pulling her face away from him so he wouldn't see the confusion in her eyes.

"You're being deliberately obtuse," Parker said from across the room, and she jerked her head up to glare at him.

"No, I'm asking a question. Nevermind. Forget it," she said with a huff, as she placed the remaining French bread on the baking pan and went to put it in the oven.

Sawyer stood leaning against the counter next to the stove with his arms crossed and a frown puckering his brow. He watched her put the tray in the oven and wipe her hands on a towel before he grabbed her wrist and pulled her in front of him.

"Why is it so hard to believe that we would pick you, baby?" he asked, and she stared at the buttons of his shirt refusing to look at his questioning eyes.

"Just forget I brought it up, the bread should be done in about ten minutes. I should probably wash up, if you'll just direct me to the bathroom?" she said quickly, pulling away from Sawyer, and turning back to the other men who all stood around the room with their arms over their chests and identical frowns on their gorgeous faces.

They exchanged looks amongst themselves, before Hudson finally broke the silence. "Come on, honey, I'll show you where it is."

He held out his hand to her, and she hesitated, drawing an exasperated huff from him, which had her quickly placing her hand in his. Drawing her along behind him, he led her out of the kitchen and back down a hallway. They stopped in front of a door, and he pushed it open. Instead of a bathroom, it was a bedroom, and she froze in the doorway.

Hudson turned back to her with a small smirk, "It's okay, Rachel, it's just my bedroom. The bathroom is right here. Right now the guest bath is torn all to hell while we're remodeling and adding on a master bedroom suite. We have four other bathrooms, but they are all connected to a bedroom. Just come back to the kitchen when you're done."

He pressed a light kiss to her forehead again, and left her standing alone in his bedroom. For just a moment she let herself breathe in his scent that filled the room. The furnishings were cherry wood, and the décor was very masculine. She could see various things that bespoke Hudson's interests scattered around.

On top of the dresser was a pile of hunting and fishing magazines while an air soft gun rested against the bedside table. Several CDs sat next to a stereo on the bookshelf, and she couldn't resist looking through them. Everything Nickelback to Five Finger Death Punch, it seemed that Hudson had an eclectic taste in his music, and that made her smile.

She remembered what she was supposed to be doing when her full bladder ached, and she hurried into the bathroom. After she finished and washed her hands, she took a moment to look over his bathroom too. It seemed too intimate to be standing amongst his things. His razor and shaving cream sat on the counter next to a bottle of cologne, a comb, and his toothbrush. She shivered thinking about how nice it might be to wake up next to him and watch him use all of it to get ready in the morning.

Stop it, Rachel. That's just crazy talk.

Her stomach twisted as she forced her mind away from thoughts of waking up in Hudson's arms long term. Very soon it wouldn't just be Hudson's arms holding her, and she wasn't sure if that scared her or excited her.

Chapter Four

Hudson, Parker, and Rogan all stopped talking to stand from the table as she returned to the kitchen, and she blushed at their manners.

"No, no, sit down. You don't have to stand for me," she scolded with a laugh.

"Our mama would have kicked our ass if we didn't stand for a woman that walked into the room," Rogan said with a smile.

"Your mama?" she asked with curiosity, as Parker held her chair for her, and then took the seat next to her. His arm snaked around the back of her chair, and she felt surrounded by his warmth.

Rogan sat on her right at the head of the table, and Hudson sat across from her. "Yes, our mama. Did you think we were hatched in the hen house? We had a mother and a father, but they died a few years back."

"I'm so sorry, I didn't mean to bring up something so sad. I remember when your father passed. The whole town turned out for the funeral service. It was a beautiful service," Rachel said, feeling guilty.

"It was a beautiful service, our mama would have approved anyway. Don't be sorry, I like that you're curious about us," Rogan said with a wink, and he reached out to lace his fingers with hers on top of the table.

"Ask all the questions you want, baby," Sawyer called from the stove, where he was finishing the sauce. She returned his easy smile, and then turned back to Rogan.

"So, can I ask what happened?" The flicker of sadness in Rogan's eyes made her ache to reach out and hug him tight.

"About seven years ago, mama got sick, and started having trouble with the muscles in her legs growing weak. She was tired all of the time, and fighting terrible headaches. It took the doctors nearly a year to diagnose that she had

Multiple Sclerosis, and unfortunately she deteriorated very quickly. When she passed, daddy just stopped living. They had been married for twenty-eight years, and he said he couldn't live without her. The doctors said it was a heart attack, but I...we believe he just died of a broken heart. He loved mama too much to keep living."

Tears filled Rachel's eyes, and before she could blink them away, one trickled down her cheek. Parker was the one to reach out and brush it away gently, and she turned to him with a small smile. "I'm sorry, I guess I just have a soft heart. How beautiful that they shared such a deep love."

Sawyer took that moment to place a large pot of spaghetti in the middle of the table, which was quickly followed by a plate of garlic bread. "Enough talk of memories, let's eat," he said, with a teasing wink at Rachel that told her he appreciated her soft heart, even if she despised it.

It didn't take long before the four Brooks brothers had her laughing so hard the tears were back in her eyes, as they joked and teased each other and her mercilessly. She could tell they loved each other and had an unbreakable bond between the four of them, and she enjoyed their camaraderie.

"How is Zoey, Rach?" She blinked at Hudson's question as she tried to formulate an answer. Zoey Carson was her best friend, and although it wasn't odd that he would ask about her, it did throw Rachel off balance.

"Uh...fine I guess. I talked to her the other day and she was busy working on her thesis."

"That's right, she's still working on her Masters in Sociology, right?"

Rachel shot Hudson a wide smile. "Yes, that's right. She wants to work in the public school system after she finishes her own education. She loves kids. We don't get to hang out as much lately between my job and her school schedule."

Parker snorted next to her, "For a long time you two were attached at the hip."

"I guess things change. I miss our girls' nights though." Rachel frowned down at her plate thinking that if Zoey hadn't been too busy to go out tonight, they probably would have stayed in and shared a bottle of wine, thus keeping her from this opportunity with the Brooks brothers.

Conversation flowed back to other townspeople and their various life circumstances. Stone River was small, and everyone seemed to know everyone else's business. It was one of the main reasons Rachel's mom had taken the job in Oklahoma, to escape the gossip.

Realizing that everyone had eaten their fill, Rachel started to stand and clear away the dishes. Parker's hand on her hip stopped her as she reached for his plate. "Sit down, sunshine. We'll get it."

"I can help," she said with a roll of her eyes.

"I said sit down," his voice took on a slightly sharper edge, and his jaw twitched. His command was so clear her body followed it without letting her brain consider it. Her butt plopped on the chair, and she grunted with irritation. His response surprised her, as he brushed a tender kiss over her lips, "Thank you, Rachel."

She watched them clear the table, and butterflies began to rumble in her stomach. Now the safety of the meal was over, the reality of what she had agreed to set in. She was about to get fucked by four men. The Brooks brothers no less. Her heart began a wild thudding in her chest, and her pussy dripped eagerly into her panties.

"Would you like another glass of wine, Rach?" Rogan asked as he pulled the bottle from the fridge. She nodded eagerly, and accepted the glass with a quiet thank you.

Taking a large gulp to steady her nerves, she caught Rogan's knowing grin, and smiled shakily back at him.

"You can relax. We aren't going to tackle you and rip your clothes off," he said, shaking his head in amusement.

She giggled when Sawyer piped up, "Unless you ask us to!"

"Shut up, jackass," Parker said smacking Sawyer upside the head.

"Just giving the lady her options. You never know, she might like it rough," he said with a shrug, and a wink in her direction. Her face blossomed into another blush, and she mentally chided herself for her reaction to them. At this rate, they were going to think she was a virgin!

Parker made his way over to the table and pulled her up into his arms gently. "Don't listen to him, sunshine. He has spent so much time fantasizing about getting you home and in his bed, that he can't help himself."

She rolled her eyes, and turned around to face Sawyer. "For the record I've never had it rough, so I don't know if I would like it or not." She was pleased she was able to pull off the haughty tone, which caused Sawyer's mouth to drop open, and his eyes to glaze over with lust.

"Fuck," Parker groaned against her ear as he wrapped an arm around her middle, and pulled her backwards against his chest. Goose bumps prickled over her skin at the intimate embrace, and his hot breath against her neck sent tendrils of fire straight to her belly.

She lifted her eyes to see that Hudson, Sawyer, and Rogan were staring at her with heated desire on their expressions, and she could feel her panties grow even damper. Moisture was building between her thighs making her shiver, and her nipples budded up into tight nubs.

Parker ran his hands up to cup her small breasts, and he gave them a gentle squeeze that drew a gasp from her. That response seemed to set him on fire, and he spun her back into his arms so quickly she collapsed against his chest with a cry.

His mouth descended on hers, and she opened for his tongue. Lightning shot through her system, igniting her entire body, and she reached up to grip his shoulders tightly, holding him close. Clutching at him like a lifeline in a hurricane.

Another body pressed against her back, and she curved her spine so her ass could grind against the thick cock there, and her breasts could still rub against Parker's chest. Soft lips pressed against the side of her neck as she kissed

Parker, and she moaned into his mouth, earning herself a quick nip on her bottom lip.

Hudson's hands that came around to the front of her shirt, and untied the knotted tails there. He tugged it gently from her shoulders leaving her in just her blinding red bra, short skirt, and black boots.

When Hudson's hands cupped her breasts from behind, she gasped again and broke off her kiss with Parker to cry out in ecstasy. Through the soft satin bra cups, she could feel the heat of his hands like a brand on her aching nipples, and she could feel something strong building deep in her womb. Stronger than she had every experienced before. She could sense the loss of control but she deftly ignored it, allowing herself the pleasure of melting into their waiting hands.

Now Rachel was panting against Parker's neck, as he suckled on her collarbone, and Hudson continued to strum her breasts like a harp. Parker bit down on the tender flesh of her shoulder, and she whimpered, her knees buckling. The two men held her up between them, and before she could react, they were moving her onto the kitchen table that just a moment ago had been set for a meal.

Lying on her back staring up at the ceiling fan in the Brooks brothers kitchen while all four of them stood over her with lust in their eyes, was better than any fantasy she had ever had in her life.

As always Parker made the first move. Tugging her skirt down over her hips, and stealing her boots along with it. Her fire engine red bra seemed to fascinate Hudson, and he gently traced his fingers around its edges, before slipping them inside to pinch her nipple. Her body jerked upward as if she had been shocked, and a warm hand on her belly pressed her back down onto the table.

Sawyer was staring down at her belly button ring like it was a lost treasure, and with an audible groan he bent to flick his tongue into the tiny cavity before teasing the dangling crystal until she whimpered. He pressed open-mouthed kisses all over her belly from hip to hip. His hot breath was erotic and soothing all at once. She tried to relax under their ministrations but found her hips rocking of their own accord, like she had no control over them at all. She felt her thong being tugged down her legs, and then she heard the sweetest words ever spoken to her.

"Fuck that is sexy," Rogan said sharply as he stood next to Parker and admired her shaved pussy. Sawyer was still focused on her belly and abdomen, and Hudson had managed to divest her of her bra. He now cupped one breast, and sucked hard on the other.

She could feel her own insecurities well up for a moment, and before she knew it, she was drawing her knees closed and moving her hands to cover her nudity.

"Hey," Hudson yelped as her nipple popped out of his mouth, "What do you think you're doing, honey?" His hands came up to the sides of her head, and he sunk his fingers into her hair to hold her still.

"I-I…" her voice cracked, and she clenched her eyes shut so he wouldn't see the tears that welled up in them.

What was she doing here? How did this all spin out of control so fast? She had four men making love to her naked body, and she was desperate for it. Like an addiction to a toxic drug, she was afraid she would never get enough of their touches.

"Rachel, tell us what's wrong? You were so hot a second ago, what happened?" Rogan's voice cut through her internal monologue, and she felt a rush of heat creep up over her cheeks and chest.

"I'm embarrassed," she whispered. When there was no response she cracked her eyes open. All four men stood gaping at her as if she had lost her mind. She closed her eyes again, praying she would wake up from this dream.

"Rachel, open your eyes," Parker demanded. He looked pleased when she complied and stared into his dark chocolate glare. "Tell us why you're feeling embarrassed."

"I've never been with more than one man, and…and…" she hesitated, but their matching looks of confusion and concern caused the words to tumble out. "I've never even had sex with the lights on. I don't like the way I look naked, and Mitch always told me that my boobs were too small. And I know my hips are a little too big—"

Sawyer's mouth cut off her rambling as he bent and kissed her long and deep. By the time he let her come up for air she was nearly panting, and she had moved her hands away from her breasts to grip his shoulders. He smiled down at her, and she smiled back.

"You have *nothing* to be ashamed of, baby. You are the sexiest woman I have ever seen in my life, and if the erections my brothers are sporting are any indication, they think so too." Sawyer's tone was serious, but his smile was playful, and his eyes were tender. She darted a glance at the others, and they each nodded their agreement.

"Rachel, let me make one thing clear," Parker said in the deep growly voice that made her pussy clench. "There isn't a damn thing about you or your body that I want to change, and I don't ever want to hear you say his name in our house again. Any man who would make his woman feel like less than a goddess when she is gifting him with her body, is an ass."

Rachel found herself giggling in spite of the gravity of his words, and she laughed harder when Parker couldn't keep his stern face straight anymore and he cracked a grin.

Rolling his eyes Parker sighed, "Do you understand what I'm saying, sunshine?"

"You're telling me to stop being self-conscious, because you want me as is," she said with another wide grin.

"Damn right I do," Parker said, and he moved back up between her thighs, "now spread your legs for me."

She did it automatically, and was rewarded by his soft praise, "Good girl." It washed over her like a soothing balm to her damaged ego, and she reached out to draw Sawyer back down to her mouth.

As she kissed Sawyer she could feel Rogan and Hudson each take up residence on opposite sides of her, and begin lavishing her body with kisses, licks, and sucks. Her brain ceased functioning the moment Parker's hot breath feathered over her dripping pussy lips.

****

Sawyer shared Rachel's breath as he kissed her with every ounce of the emotions rolling through his body. The idea that this gorgeous, strong woman would feel insecure in front of him and his brothers completely blew his mind. He had been half in love with her for the last five years, and now that he had tasted her, and held her in his arms, there was no way he could go back. It would be impossible to let her go.

Her mouth dropped open underneath his in a gasp of delight, and he turned so he could see the top of Parker's dark head moving between her beautiful white thighs. His mouth watered at the idea of tasting her sweet cream.

Sawyer tore his gaze away from Parker eating her pussy when her hands cupped the back of his neck, and his shoulder, alternately gripping and clawing at his shirt. He tugged the offending material over his head and dropped it on the floor, relieved to have another barrier out from between them. Rachel's smile of pleasure as her gaze roamed over his naked chest sent his ego skyrocketing to the moon.

He held still while she ran her hands over his pecks and down to the fly of his jeans, but when she groaned and her hands fumbled with the buttons, he took over and removed them too. Parker was keeping her on the edge of orgasm, and Rogan and Hudson were teasing and tempting every inch of her naked flesh they could reach.

"Oh yes!" she moaned as her hips rocked and thrust against Parker's face.

Her moan was like gasoline on Sawyer's already burning libido, so he reached out and cupped her cheek, turning her to face his rock hard erection. When she licked her lips and her gaze focused on his cock, he lost every bit of control he had. He pressed his angry red cockhead against her soft pink lips, and she automatically opened for him. Her hot little tongue ran over the bottom ridge of his corona, and he clenched his teeth fighting against an early orgasm.

"Holy shit," he gasped, and his brain went fuzzy. His hips pressed forward automatically, and he was surprised to find she opened her jaw to him easily. She didn't gag, or choke as his cockhead found the back of her throat. She actually seemed to become more turned on the deeper he slid into her, and he watched in awe as she hollowed her cheeks and sucked him deeply down her throat. Her throat muscles tightened around his sensitive crown and he felt his balls tighten up. "You're going to kill me."

He very nearly embarrassed himself by shooting his wad down her throat before she had even come once, but she let go of him when her body arched violently up from the table. A quick glance down showed him that Parker had a couple of fingers thrust into her pussy, and was sucking hard on her clit.

Parker released her clit long enough to say, "Come for me, Rachel."

With that demand echoing around them, she seemed to explode. Her body jerked and thrashed, and a red hot blush covered her from her sweaty forehead to her beaded nipples. Her eyes were clenched tightly shut, and her mouth gaped open as she screamed out Parker's name.

It was magnificent, and Sawyer felt his heart swell. He wanted to spend the rest of his life watching this woman reach her climax under his and his brothers' hands. A moment of guilt shot through him that they hadn't been completely honest with her when they convinced her to come out here.

The four of them had had many a conversation regarding Rachel Morgan, and every scenario they imagined ended with her accepting them as a unit and living happily ever after. Now that they had the opportunity, they were on a mission to convince her the five of them could make this work.

Parker finally raised his head, and his heavy lidded eyes were filled with lust. Sawyer could see Rachel's juices covering his chin and lips, and again he wondered how she tasted. Deciding he couldn't wait any longer, he moved away from his position by her head until he stood next to Parker between her thighs.

"Damn, that's a beautiful sight," he murmured softly as he stared down at the prettiest pale pink pussy he had ever seen. She was completely shaved, and her tiny clit was beaded up begging to be played with. Her pussy lips were swollen, and dripping with cream. "My turn, baby."

Sliding one finger through her folds, he caught her desire filled gaze, and he lifted his finger to his mouth to suck the juice off. She moaned at the sight, and he smiled down at her with a quick wink.

Dropping to his knees between her spread thighs, the hot musky scent of female fogged his brain further. He was vaguely aware of Rogan moving up beside her head to give her access to his cock. Her little pointed pink tongue darted out to lick the moisture from Rogan's dick, and Sawyer's own cock jerked in response.

Blocking out what was happening at the head of the table, he focused on the juicy slit in front of him. With his thumbs he spread her plump pussy lips wide, and ran his tongue through her cream. Her clit throbbed with her pulse, and he could feel her muscles clenching as he thrust his tongue inside of her. The sweet flavor of her cream sent fire snaking through his body, and he had to squeeze the base of his own cock to regain his control.

Close to embarrassing himself, he stood and reached for the condoms that one of his brothers had dropped on a chair. He ripped it open with his teeth and covered his aching cock as quickly as he dared. With protection in place, he placed the head of his dick against her moist pussy, and pressed forward.

The moment he began to sink into her hot body, was like reaching heaven's gates, and seeing them open to welcome him. Her back bowed up, and she released Rogan's cock as her mouth dropped open wide, and she cried out. Sawyer's balls tightened at the sound of his name on her lips, and he stopped his forward motion for a moment to let her adjust around him. The tight muscles were fluttering inside her body, and he knew he didn't have long before he wouldn't be able hold his climax back.

She reached out with her hands, and pressed against his chest as if to hold him back as she twisted her hips a little, fine-tuning the position so she could accommodate his size. Once her hands relaxed, Sawyer looked up at Parker who always seemed to lead the way in these encounters. Parker reached for her hands pulling them back up over her head where Rogan was now waiting to hold them to the table.

The position opened her entire body to their view, and left her vulnerable to their every whim. Sawyer could hear the hitch in her breathing, and a flash of insecurity went through her eyes. He gave her what he hoped was a reassuring smile, and thrust another inch into her.

"Oh my God!" she cried out, throwing her head back, and clenching her hands into fists. Rogan didn't let go of her wrists, and Sawyer could see every muscle in her body grow taut.

Hudson and Parker exchanged a look and a nod, before they each took up residence on opposite sides of her body. Bending, they each took a nipple into their mouths, and judging by Rachel's instant clenching motion on Sawyer's cock he was assuming they bit down on those sensitive buds.

Using the distraction to his advantage, he thrust the rest of the way into her body, and he could feel his cockhead hit her cervix just as his balls slapped against her ass.

"Holy fuck you're tight, baby," he moaned, letting his own head fall back, as he relished the molten heat that enveloped him.

"Please, Sawyer!" she groaned, and Parker lifted his head.

Parker's eyes flashed, and Sawyer bit his bottom lip, knowing his brother would want to hear more than her pretty pleas. Sawyer barely heard him over the pounding of his own heart, as Parker instructed her, "Please what, Rachel? Tell him what you need."

"I need…move, please…I need you to move." She writhed underneath them so violently that Sawyer had to grab ahold of her hips to keep his position in her cunt.

Using his hands to hold her in place, he began slowly retreating and thrusting forward. He was desperately trying to maintain his control over his own needs so he could bring her the most pleasure possible. Suddenly, she began bucking like a wildcat underneath him.

"Please, Sawyer, harder!" she begged, and his control snapped. Slamming his hips forward he fucked her. He plowed into her, enjoying the way she pushed her pussy against him begging for more without saying a word.

His orgasm was like hitting a wall of fire when it broke inside of him. He could feel the jets of cum spewing from him into the condom, and her pussy tightened like a vice around his cock as she reached another orgasm.

The sound of her screaming out his name was the best thing his ears had ever heard. Until Rogan released her arms and she wrapped around Sawyer, burying her face into his throat, and whispering his name again. That moment his heart melted, and she owned him body and soul. Whether or not she knew it, understood it, or accepted it, he would always love the little spitfire that gave her body to him so willingly, and with so much passion.

Chapter Five

Rachel's world was tilted on its axis by her second orgasm, and she was having a hard time bringing it back to center. Sawyer's cock was still buried deep inside of her, and he was slumped over her body, wrapped in her arms. She loved the sweaty, sticky feeling of his muscular chest against her tender breasts.

"Wow," she whispered, and all four men chuckled.

"Are you alright, baby?" Sawyer asked, kissing her on the nose as he brushed the hair away from her face.

"Hell yes. I'm fantastic!" His satisfied grin made her giggle. "I think I just saw stars for a minute there."

"Aww, cut that out. He's going to get a big head if you keep stroking his ego," Hudson said as Sawyer gently pulled free of her body.

"Mmmm....after that performance he's allowed," she moaned, stretching her muscles, and arching her back. Lying on their kitchen table naked and glowing with her orgasms, she felt sexier than she had ever felt in her life. Hudson stroked his hand over her belly causing the muscles there to twitch in anticipation, and his eyes sparked with amusement.

"There's more to come, if you're up for it." Her eyes met Hudson's, and when she nodded, his smile lit up his face. Bending forward he claimed her mouth in a deep kiss. His tongue stroked hers and she had the distinct feeling he was trying to memorize her flavor. As he broke off the kiss, he whispered breathlessly, "Pinch me."

"What?" She tipped her head back and frowned up into his dark brown eyes.

"Pinch me, honey. I'm not sure this is real. I've been dreaming about getting my hands on you for so long, that I'm afraid I'll wake up and this will be a dream," he said softly, and she could hear his brothers groaning at his sweet words.

She ignored them, and tugged him down until their foreheads rested against each other.

"You aren't dreaming, cowboy, but if you don't get to it, you might miss your opportunity. Your brothers are still waiting for their turn," she whispered loudly, causing him to laugh as he scooped her up in his arms off the table.

"Well if I'm going to make my fantasies come true I'm not doing it on the kitchen table. I want you in my bed," he said as he stalked through the house with her in his arms. She found herself spread out on his bed a moment later, and she glanced up as Rogan and Parker followed them into the room. Rogan had removed his shirt earlier, and his pants were unzipped from her sucking his cock, but both Hudson and Parker were fully clothed.

Her frown must have caught Rogan's attention, "What's wrong, Rach?"

"Why am I the only one naked?" she asked with a small pout.

"You're not, I'm naked too, and if these dumbasses don't get busy, I'll be warming those sheets with you again," Sawyer said as he came through the bedroom doorway, still naked and with a semi-hard erection again.

She laughed as Hudson ripped his clothes off like a wild man, while Rogan and Parker removed theirs more deliberately. The two oldest brothers seemed content to let Hudson take his turn without interference, and they both stood back watching as Hudson moved between her legs. She willingly spread them wide, and held her arms out to him in welcome. He took her mouth again in a gentle kiss that promised he would be a sweet and sensitive lover.

His fingers skimmed over her lower belly, and then down to the top of her slit. When he reached the dripping moisture there, he groaned against her tongue, and pushed his finger deeper into her folds.

Pushing her hips up, she encouraged him to go as far as he could, before he pulled back and rubbed her clit with little circles until it was once again throbbing with need. Her thigh muscles were twitching as she gripped him tighter to her, and he ran the head of his cock through her juices getting it nice and wet.

She jumped when she felt him rub the tip of it against her tight asshole, and his eyes shot to hers. She knew her shock and apprehension showed on her face, because he smiled reassuringly and began to press his dick into her wet cunt.

"Has anyone ever had the pleasure of fucking that sweet ass, honey?" he asked her as she thrust her hips up to meet him. She nodded her head, and heard three corresponding sighs of relief from nearby. "Good, that makes things simpler."

Before she could formulate a response to his words, he was slamming his cock in and out of her vibrating body with a force that was quickly going to send her spiraling out of control. Her cries of delight echoed throughout the room, along with their heavy breathing, and his groans. Hudson's cock filled her up as fully as Sawyer's had, and she clenched her muscles around him trying to keep him inside of her. With his hiss of breath encouraging her, she clawed at his muscular arms where they were braced beside her hips, and rocked her hips up to meet his every movement. She could feel her breasts bouncing with the rhythm, but she still squealed in surprised when Rogan moved to her side and captured one of her nipples in his mouth.

Her hand slid into Rogan's short hair and held him close while he feasted on the puckered nub. Eyes clenched shut, the pleasure overwhelmed her, and she screamed out Hudson's name, crashing through the barrier to find yet another release. She felt his dick jerking inside of her and he gripped her hips, holding her against him while his cum filled the condom he was wearing.

For just a brief flash, she wondered what it would feel like to be full of his cum, to feel him dripping from between her thighs as she moved. A shudder of desire rumbled through her body, and she sighed heavily.

With her eyes still closed, she focused on the movements around her. Hudson lifted himself away from her body, but not before giving her a tender kiss and nuzzle on her exposed throat. Parker and Rogan seemed to move in unison, climbing onto the bed on either side of her, and shifting her to her side. When she felt one hard cock press against her pubic bone, and another between her ass cheeks, she inhaled sharply and her eyes popped open.

"What—" she started to protest, but Parker's gentle nip on her shoulder cut her off.

"Shhh...Rachel we both want you, but you're so responsive that you're going to wear yourself out before we all have an opportunity. Haven't you ever wondered what it would feel like to have a hard cock in your ass, while another is fucking your pussy?" Rogan whispered to her.

She stared into his dark brown eyes seeing emotions she wasn't ready to handle there. The truth was she had always fantasized about a ménage, but fear had kept her from attempting it. She had always assumed that anal sex was more for the man's pleasure than the woman's, because the few experiences she had had with it weren't fantastic. But Rogan was offering her both. He wanted to pleasure her, while Parker took his pleasure in her ass.

Another thought occurred to her just as she was getting ready to nod her agreement. "Won't you be able to feel each other? Isn't that a little weird?"

She heard Parker chuckle behind her, but Rogan just smiled down at her. "Yes, we can feel each other via you, but I promise you there will be skin separating us, and neither of us will be focused on each other. Only you, sexy. We want to bring you the ultimate pleasure."

She hesitated, but Parker gripped her chin and turned her so she could see him. "Sunshine, we won't hurt you. I promise. Let us make you feel good."

There was honesty in his eyes, and she wanted so desperately in that moment to please him that she would have done anything. Nodding her agreement, she saw his slow smile as he murmured, "Good, girl. Now, kiss Rogan while I play with you to get you ready."

Rogan didn't waste any time capturing her mouth with his. He ravished her, suckling her tongue and biting her lip gently. There wasn't a crevice in her mouth he missed, and when he finished exploring, he started over again. It was a good thing he was so intent on distracting her, because she hadn't even noticed Parker retrieving some lube and rubbing it against her asshole, until he pressed his finger into the tight ring of muscles.

She instinctively clenched down on his finger and pushed against him. It was a foreign discomfort, but she didn't feel any pain. Awkwardly, she froze in her kissing of Rogan while she tried to grasp the rainbow of sensations Parker's finger was causing in her rectum. He pressed in and out at a slow, gentle pace for a few thrusts before he added a second finger to the motion and stretched her further. A slight burning pinch was followed by a wave of intense pleasure as Rogan thrust his two fingers into her dripping pussy. Simultaneously pleasured from both sides, she moaned loudly.

"That's it, sunshine. Tell us what you like," Parker murmured against her ear with a little growl, before spreading his fingers wide stretching her tight passage. "I'm going to fuck this little ass, and you're going to beg me not to stop."

"Please! Parker! Rogan!" she gasped each word out on every thrust of their fingers, and lifted her leg up and over Rogan's hip, opening her wider to their touch.

Rogan wasted no time in rubbing his condom-covered cock in her juices and pushing his way into her pussy. Her cunt was like a greedy glove sucking him in and trying to hold him close. After a few shallow thrusts, he managed to sink completely into her, and she shivered with anticipation as Parker's lubed up cock pressed gently but firmly against her tender asshole.

Instead of pushing into her right away, Parker reached around and pinched her clit hard. It fuzzed her brain nearly sending her into another orgasm. The moment her muscles relaxed from their tense state, he pressed the head of his cock into her, forcing his way past the tight circle with a grunt. Suddenly he stopped, and she let out all of the air in her lungs in one solid whoosh.

Before she had a chance to ask questions, Rogan was withdrawing from her and Parker was easing the rest of the way into her channel. He slid in much smoother this time, and she let out a low moan.

"I'm in," Parker said in a tight, husky voice.

That was Rogan's cue, and he wasted no time pushing back into her tight pussy. She pressed back against Parker and tried to relax as both men found their way into her body. They held completely still for a couple of heartbeats to let her adjust to them, and she had to admit she was enjoying the feeling of Rogan's cock pressing against her G-spot, while Parker's filled her backside. The sensation of fullness was so strong she felt herself choking for air, and she dug her fingernails into Rogan's biceps. Throwing her head back onto Parker's shoulder, she clenched her eyes shut against the onslaught of their loving.

Rogan cupped her breasts in his hands, pinching and twisting her nipples slightly, while Parker's fingers gripped her hips holding her in place for his focused thrusts. Like a seesaw, they set up a rhythm that drove her toward a monster climax she wasn't sure she would survive. Giving up resisting the sensations, she clenched down on the two cocks embedded in her body, and released herself to the orgasm that had built.

She heard her own scream of pleasure as though from a distance, just before Parker and Rogan jointly thrust into her body and let themselves come. She rested her forehead against Rogan's collarbone while Parker pressed a kiss to the nape of her neck.

"That was…" she stopped trying to come up with just the right word for what that was.

"Phenomenal?"

"Sexy as fuck?"

"Amazing?"

"Only the beginning."

"Perfect," she finished with a giggle at their suggestions. "It was perfect. I can't wait to do it again."

Rogan laughed, and kissed her forehead. "Aw shit, we've created a monster."

"That's one monster I don't mind feeding. I think we'll keep her," Hudson said from nearby. Rachel lifted her head to eyeball him because he sounded serious about keeping her. His shrug and wink reassured her that he was still his playful self, and she sighed heavily. Arching her back she gave a little wiggle and heard two masculine groans of appreciation.

"I have to agree, it was pretty damn perfect and, sunshine, if you keep that up, you'll be doing it again in no time," Parker murmured against her temple.

A shiver of lust shot through her, and she bit her lip. She had just had multiple mind-blowing orgasms, and yet her pussy gripped Rogan's cock like a handcuff. She could feel the craving for them building inside of her again, and she mentally shook herself. If this kept up she would lose herself to them and get hurt when it was time to say goodbye. Instead of thinking about the inevitable moment of completion, she looked up into Rogan's eyes and smiled.

Chapter Six

"So what's for dessert?" she asked with a wicked grin.

"Hmm...I think we should just turn you into dessert," Rogan said, kissing her nose before he slid out of her body, and went to deal with the used condom. Parker was right behind him, leaving her exposed from the back as well. She wasn't cold for more than a second, before Hudson and Sawyer were filling their places.

"Rogan, if you had tasted her, you would already know she's sweeter than any dessert," Sawyer said while he nuzzled his face into her hair from behind. She felt a blush creep up her cheeks that triggered another round of laughter from the brothers.

"Are you hungry, honey?" Hudson asked, looking more seriously at her.

"Well, you guys did just work my ass out."

"Damn right I did," Parker said with an arrogant smirk as he brought a washcloth out of the bathroom. She was shocked when Hudson moved out of the way, and Parker reached for her.

She jerked away from him rolling to her back. "What are you doing?"

"I was just going to clean you up. Is that a problem?" his eyes narrowed into a frown.

"Why? I can do it." She was puzzled. She knew she was less experienced than they were, but she had never heard of a man taking the time to wash his partner after sex unless it was in the shower.

"Because I want to, and you deserve to be cared for." He waited patiently with his hand on her upper thigh, unwavering from his request.

When she finally relented and gave him a nod, his look of approval melted her insides. His eyes never left hers, and his touch between her thighs was gentle as he wiped the evidence of their loving away from her skin. To her surprise the gesture felt completely natural, as if she had felt it a thousand times, and anticipated feeling it a thousand more. His large hands handled her like a delicate piece of china, but she remembered distinctly the strength they had had when he gripped her hips. A little rush of moisture flooded her pussy, and she felt her cheeks light up with a blush as his eyebrow raised in question.

"You need to eat again, sunshine, before we take care of the problem you seem to have there," Parker said as he finished wiping her clean, and went back to the bathroom.

She shivered when the cool temperature of the room chilled her damp nether regions, and turned her attention back to the other three Brooks brothers. Rogan and Hudson had both managed to pull jeans on, but Sawyer still reclined beside her, deliciously nude.

"Sawyer, as much as I enjoy the view, if you don't get dressed I might just jump you again," she said, playfully running her finger down the indentation in the center of his six-pack abs.

"Fuck that. Go ahead and jump me, baby. I'm all yours," he said, wiggling his eyebrows.

Rogan suddenly scooped her up from the bed drawing a startled yelp from her. "No you don't. You need a little break. We are far from done playing with you, but I want you to last through the whole weekend, and besides, if you're going to jump anyone, it should be me."

He stood her on her feet next to a large chest of drawers and quickly pulled out a white t-shirt. Smiling, he tugged it over her arms and down to cover her nudity, before he stepped back to take in the view. From nearby Hudson whistled, and Sawyer groaned.

"What?" she asked curiously.

"Ever heard that song by Keith Urban? The one that says "you look good in my shirt"?" Hudson's eyes had darkened with heat, and she felt lust coil in her belly.

Rogan ran his hand down her arm, before brushing a lock of her brown hair away from her eyes. "Oh yeah, I have never seen anyone look so good in a plain white shirt."

Rachel shifted uncomfortably, and wrinkled her nose, "Okay enough of that. I don't need pretty words—"

"You need to eat, and rest," Parker's commanding tone cut off her words as he pushed Rogan out of the way and grabbed her hand. Spinning her around so she faced the door, he directed her out of the bedroom. She could hear the curses and grumblings of his three brothers as he stole her from their presence and led her into the living room. "But, Rachel, if we want to whisper pretty words to you, you need to just enjoy them."

She rolled her eyes as he set her down on her feet next to the sofa. His sigh of frustration was loud and clear. "Sit down."

She flinched. "I'm not a dog, Parker!"

The muscle in his jaw twitched as he clenched his teeth. She could tell he wasn't used to being disobeyed when he gave a command, but she was ridiculously pleased when he finally said, "Please sit."

She hesitated before letting out a loud huff and plopping down onto the sofa.

"Thank you, sunshine. We'll discuss punishment for your attitude later." He winked at her as he left the room, and she snapped her gaping mouth shut. Sawyer and Rogan stood in the doorway with matching grins on their faces, while Hudson followed Parker to the kitchen.

"What did he mean by that?" she asked, but only got shrugs in response.

"Who knows? Parker is a special kind of guy," Sawyer said as he sat down next to her and pulled her into his lap.

She knew she should probably resist just to keep some distance between them, but her body instinctively snuggled into his broad chest. His warm masculine scent filled her nose and she let it sink into her brain. She felt so comfortable in his arms. It was like she was meant to be there. A twinge of unease niggled at her brain. She was getting too close to these guys. If she let herself, she could easily fall in love with the four Brooks brothers, and that would get her hurt. Her entire body tensed at the thought, and Sawyer noticed.

"What's wrong, baby?" he asked, frowning down at her. His arms were still wrapped around her, with one hand resting on the outside of her upper thigh, and the other cupping her butt. With his naked chest pressed against her cheek, she could feel his heartbeat pick up speed at her silence.

"Nothing. I'm good," she whispered, running her fingers over the small patch of hair between his nipples.

"What happened with Mitch?"

Parker's voice was loud in her ears as he came back into the room carrying a tray. The awkward question wasn't one she had any interest in answering. Especially not when telling the truth would point out her flaws to the four men she had just had mind-blowing sex with.

"None of your business," she snapped without moving from her place in Sawyers arms. He seemed to freeze underneath her, and she tilted her head to look up at him. His eyes were suddenly jumping between her and Parker, and it made her very uncomfortable.

"Rachel, I'm going to ask you again, and this time it would be in your best interest if you answered me with a little more respect. What happened with Mitch?" Ice laced Parker's voice now, and it tweaked at the feminist in her. Why did he have to ruin the moment by turning into an arrogant asshole?

"Respect this, Parker, Mitch is none of your fucking business. What happened between us happened, and it's over now. I'm here with you, but I won't be for much longer if you don't get off your goddamn high horse and stop treating me like I'm a child." She stood and moved toward the hallway door with every intention of getting showered and getting dressed to leave. Rogan's hand shot out and latched onto her wrist stopping her before she made it that far. The temperature in the room dropped at least fifteen degrees as she stood glaring at Parker, who just glared back in that domineeringly sexy way. *Why the hell does he have to be so hot when he is being so bossy?*

"Rachel, he just wants to know if we need to go kick Mitch's ass for hurting you," Rogan said, easing his grip and stroking his thumb over the pulse in her wrist.

She jerked her head over to stare at him in surprise, and then looked back to Parker who hadn't moved a muscle. "Is that true?"

His only acknowledgement was a sharp nod, and she immediately warmed inside. That certainly changed things. Pulling her wrist from Rogan's loosened grip, she took two large steps and leapt up into Parker's arms locking her legs around his waist, and pressing her bare pussy against his naked abs. Like he was actually expecting it, he caught her with ease, and wrapped one arm around her waist while his other arm went under her ass to support her. She pressed a hot kiss to his open mouth, sucking his tongue into hers, and pushed all of the passion, gratitude, and desire she had for him into the kiss. He responded instantly, squeezing her tightly, and groaning against her mouth.

"Well hell, if I had known bossing her around would get her all worked up like that, I would have tried it myself," Sawyer grumbled behind her from his place on the couch.

She tore her mouth away from Parker, panting hard and enjoying the blazing lust that glowed in his eyes. "Thank you."

The muscles in his jaw softened just a little bit, and his lip quirked up, "Sunshine, you're sexy as fuck when you get all high and mighty. Makes me want to paddle your ass until it's red hot."

Rachel swallowed hard as her pussy creamed at the mental image of him spanking her ass. "I will have to make sure I disobey you regularly."

The wicked grin that spread across his face, and the matching groans from his three brothers, made her laugh. It was a whole body laugh as she tossed her head back and just let the joy of these four men fill her up. Parker settled into a chair with her straddling his lap, and his thick cock pressing his zipper against her clit.

"Mmmm...you don't feel like you want to eat right now," she said, trailing kisses down his throat.

"Well, I want to eat right now, honey, but it ain't this ice cream I want to eat," Hudson said from behind her.

"Ice cream?" She stopped what she was doing and twisted to see three pairs of desire-filled eyes focused on her ass where the t-shirt had ridden up. "Hey, eyes up top!"

Laughing, Rogan reached for the tray of bowls, and waved one at her. "Come here, sexy. I know you have a weakness for ice cream, and I will happily share mine."

Parker swatted her ass gently as she climbed out of his lap to move over to Rogan, and she flashed him a grin. Turning back to his older brother, she frowned. "Hey, why are there only four bowls?"

Rogan just grinned and waved a spoon at her. "I told you I would share, come here, Rach."

When she was settled on his lap, he held up a spoonful of vanilla ice cream for her, and she grinned. "Where's the chocolate syrup and whipped cream?"

"I'll give you cream, baby," Sawyer muttered under his breath, while Hudson handed over a bottle of chocolate syrup. Rogan quickly added it to the bowl of ice cream and the spoon before lifting it to her lips.

"Open wide," he teased, and this time she obeyed without hesitation. As soon as the ice cream hit her tongue, her eyes drifted shut and she sighed.

"Mmm...that's good," she moaned with pleasure. "How did you guys know I have a soft spot for ice cream."

Parker snorted, "Sunshine, everyone in town knows how often you visit the ice cream shop. I believe you have a particular affinity to the Chocolate Mountain flavor, or at least that's what flavor I've seen you with."

"Yeah, Dotty actually created that flavor just for me, because I love chocolate so much." She sat in Rogan's lap staring across the room at Parker with wide eyes. It was astonishing to her that these guys knew her that well. If someone had asked her yesterday about the four Brooks brothers, she would have simply explained they were friends, but not close friends. Apparently, they were closer to her than she thought.

"Your ice cream is melting, Rach," Rogan said softly, holding another spoonful up to her parted lips. She took the bite, and then licked her lips with pleasure.

Rogan's eyes followed the movement of her tongue, and his pupils dilated. She could feel this cock thicken under her ass, and she squirmed a little enjoying his sharp hiss of breath. His fist tightened on the handle of the spoon as he dipped more of the sweet concoction for her. It was really quite decadent to be sitting half-naked on his lap while he hand fed her. Add to the fact his three equally sexy brothers sat nearby watching and waiting for their turn to share with her, and it melted her mind. Her clit started to throb, and she shifted her position, drawing a groan from Rogan.

He continued to feed her the ice cream, and she made sure to tease and taunt him with every lick of the spoon. Just as the spoon jingled in the bowl signaling the end of the erotic interlude, she slid from his lap to the floor between his knees.

"What are you doing, sexy?" Rogan's jaw was clenched, and his abs were drawn up tight with tension. She could see the fat mushroom head of his cock sticking up over the top of his blue jeans, and her mouth watered.

"Thanking you for sharing your dessert," she whispered as she slid his zipper down carefully so as not to maim his twitching cock.

"Fuck," he groaned as she darted her tongue out to lap at the drop of pre-cum glistening on top of his erection.

"Not yet, Rogan, be patient," she murmured, licking her way down his cock to his balls and back up. Opening her mouth as wide as she could, she slid her lips over his length, sucking hard as he hit her tonsils.

The sound of his heavy breathing echoed in her head, and she forgot about everything except the feeling and taste of his thick dick in her mouth. She couldn't quite take him all the way down her throat, so she added her hands to the mix, and began a squeezing twisting motion in combination with her sucking. Pressing her tongue up against the sensitive spot just below the corona of his cock, she hummed softly, and nearly laughed when he cursed again.

The large vein on the underside of his prick started throbbing, and she pulled back to tease the head a little more. Apparently that didn't suit his current plan, because he slid his hand into her long hair, and gripped her tightly. Directing her head downward, he thrust up to meet her. Relaxing her jaw so she could take more of him, she let him face fuck her.

Her eyes opened to watch him, and met his dark brown gaze as he watched. A shiver of lust stroked through her at the need she saw on his face. Swallowing hard, she began a hard sucking motion as he thrust between her lips, and with a shout, his cum began shooting into her mouth. Refusing to lose a drop, she tightened her lips, and swallowed every bit of his cream, enjoying the feeling of feminine accomplishment as he dropped his head back onto the chair and sighed heavily. She didn't release his cock until it stopped twitching, and she sat back on her haunches. Rogan tugged his hand free of her hair, and stroked it down her cheek with a wink that made her blush.

Chapter Seven

"Damn. I want to share next," Hudson said in a husky voice from behind her. She jumped a little at the reminder of their audience, and giggled.

"Only if you have ice cream," she responded with a laugh, as Rogan lifted her up and into his lap.

She settled her head in the crook of his neck and inhaled his spicy male scent deeply, enjoying the feeling of his fingers running up and down her arm and leg, and his wide chest pillowing her body. Before she could stop herself she yawned widely, and Rogan chuckled.

"Our girl is damn near asleep, boys. I think it's time to give her a little rest."

Rachel lifted her head and looked around at the other brothers. No one seemed upset at all, and she breathed a little sigh of relief. "I'm sorry, guys. It's been awhile since I've had more than one orgasm in a night, and I lost count of how many I had tonight. I think Rogan's right, I need some sleep."

"Rachel, don't ever be sorry to tell us what you need," Parker answered with a frown. He stood and moved to her side, reaching for her. She went willingly, and he began leading her back down the hallway toward the bedrooms.

They bypassed Hudson's room this time, and went into another across the hall. She was surprised to find herself in what was clearly Rogan's room. He had the same bedframe as Hudson, but his room was neat as a pin. There was very little clutter scattered on top of the dresser and nightstand, and the sheets were even turned down at the head of the bed awaiting its nightly occupant. She giggled at the pair of slippers she saw peeking out from under the edge, and then jumped when Hudson spoke in her ear.

"Yeah, he's a bit of a neat freak. The rest of us aren't so much, that's why Parker brought you in here. We'll have to make do with switching rooms until we get the master suite finished. Then we'll have more space."

Rachel flashed him a smile. "It has a bed and a pillow so it will work perfectly for my needs tonight. So which one of you is a cuddler?"

"That would be me, baby. I'm a spooner," Sawyer said, stepping into the bedroom behind Hudson. Rogan followed, and she was again surrounded by large muscular bodies.

It's like I'm in heaven.

Shaking off the lust that kept fuzzing her brain, she patted Sawyer's chest. "Good to know. You have to sleep in another bed, because I need my own zip code when I sleep."

He looked shocked, and his brothers were all laughing. "What?"

"Yep, sorry, big guy. I am *not* a cuddler. In fact, I'm kind of a bed hog, so whomever is brave enough to share the bed with me, gets what he deserves." She turned and walked away from them, not wanting to be a part of the discussion over who would share her bed. That wasn't a choice she could make. Reaching the doorway to the bathroom, she turned back, "I'm going to wash up before I sleep. I'll just be a minute."

No one said anything, so she went into the bathroom and shut the door behind her. She rested her back against it and stared at herself in the mirror over the sink. The woman staring back was tousled and looked like she had been well loved. Her hair was in wild curls around her head, and there was a small love bite on her throat. Swollen lips were reddened, and her eyes were slightly glassy. A whisker burn ran down the inside of one thigh, and she grinned remembering how it got there. Never before had she felt so affected by anyone.

It was a pity that it was four men instead of just one, because there was no future in this weekend of pleasure. Her stomach dipped as she thought about leaving Sunday. How would she handle seeing them around town? Or God forbid seeing them with another woman at the bar? This whole charade was going to blow up in her face, she had no doubt, and yet she couldn't bring herself to leave. She wanted to suck the joy out of every possible moment she could so later she could look back on this weekend and smile.

Straightening her spine, she washed up, and ran her fingers through her hair. There was a change of clothes in her bag, but she wasn't interested in taking off Hudson's t-shirt. It felt too perfect to want to remove it. Blocking out the reasons she shook herself mentally because she wasn't ready to examine those feelings.

When she opened the bedroom door, she was stunned to find Rogan and Parker both in the room waiting for her. "Seriously, guys? I wasn't joking. I'm not the best sleeping partner."

Rogan grinned and Parker shook his head, "Sunshine, we're putting you in the middle, that way we can rein you in when we need to. Don't worry about the two of us, we'll be fine."

She sighed and shrugged, "Okay, but if you hit the floor in the middle of the night, don't blame me."

They were settled into the bed in a few moments, and she lay on her back staring at the ceiling with a man on either side of her watching her. It was awkward. What was she supposed to say?

"You're overthinking," Rogan said softly.

The darkness hid the ever-present blush that heated her cheeks, and she turned her head to look at him. She couldn't see the definition of his face, only his silhouette, but she knew he was completely focused on her right now.

"Tell me why four brothers would ever want to share a woman amongst them?" she asked quietly, expecting them to deny her.

Parker sighed heavily, and ran his hand down her arm to lace his fingers with hers. "I can't speak for the others, but for me it's something I struggled with when we first started talking about it. I have very strong dominant tendencies—"

"What? You? No way!" Rachel feigned a shocked gasp and lifted their clenched hands to her chest while Rogan laughed.

"Okay, so I'm a Dominant. It's not something I do intentionally. It's just part of my makeup. But as I was saying, having the need to be in control went completely against the idea of a ménage. It's not like my three brothers are going to stand back and wait for me to direct all of the action, so I wasn't sure I could make it work."

"What changed your mind?"

"My dad withered away and died because of a broken heart after mama died. I couldn't stop thinking about what it would have been like for her if she had been alive when he died and suddenly found herself alone. A ménage relationship protects our woman from being completely alone. If something tragic were to happen to one of us, there would be three of us left behind to help console her and make sure she was still loved and protected."

Rachel was silent while she listened to Parker's reasoning. She was stunned at the depth of emotion she could hear in his voice. He was serious. He wanted a ménage relationship so his woman would always be cared for. It was deeply touching, and it made her heart warm. He might be a bossy prick on occasion, but there was more under the surface yet to be explored.

Rogan spoke up before Rachel could voice her opinion, "For me it stems from the fact I love and respect my brothers, and we all seem to have the same taste in women. I don't see any reason for limitations on love, and I believe people can love more than one person at a time. I figure if we find the one woman, with a big enough heart, and a strong enough spine to tolerate all four of us, then we should tie her to the bed and never let her go."

A laugh broke free from her throat, and she reached her other hand up to cup Rogan's cheek. "I'm not sure that's the best way to propose it to a woman, but good luck."

"Why does ménage intimidate you, but my dominance doesn't, Rachel?" Parker's question was a valid one, and she took a minute to think about it.

"There are moments when you can be over-the-top bossy, but usually your demands, or requests if you want to call them, are to my benefit. I can't say I'm perfectly submissive, but I'm happy to let a man lead in the bedroom. Don't get me wrong, I'm not exactly into pain, so I don't know if I could ever be a legitimate sub and get my ass beat," she said trying to sound serious, but smiling anyway.

"Okay, so you don't want a twenty-four seven relationship with a Dom, but that doesn't tell us why ménage scares you so much," Rogan responded.

"Ménage doesn't scare me, I guess…it's the relationship part that scares me." When they were both silent at her admission, she grew nervous. "I just haven't had any luck with committed relationships. You saw what Mitch did to me, and he's not the first guy that's cheated on me. In fact, I haven't had a single relationship with a man where I didn't get hurt. My own father took off when I was just eight years old after he fell in love with his office assistant, and I watched my mom attempt to date over and over through the years only to get hurt in some way every time. You have to understand I just don't want to get hurt again."

"So you're going to avoid relationships forever?" Rogan asked, and Rachel frowned up at his darkened profile.

"No I guess not. I don't know. Right now, I just don't know what I want."

Silence reigned after that, and Rachel found she was completely comfortable just lying there holding their hands in the quiet of the night. It was an oddly cathartic experience. Neither man judged her for her opinions, or for the fact that Mitch had cheated on her. They didn't push her to make decisions she wasn't ready to make, or question her about things she wasn't ready to talk about. They just listened and absorbed it all.

****

It wasn't long before the weight of sleep swallowed her, and Parker lay staring down at her while she slept. His hand was still laced with hers and resting on her rib cage where he could feel the even keel of her breathing, and the thud of her heart. A heart that had been damaged, yet longing for love.

He knew his brothers shared his attraction and fascination with Rachel, but until this moment, he had never expected to find himself falling in love with her too. He admired her spunk and her determination. She fought for what she wanted, yet knew when the right time to back down was as well.

This little five foot tall wildcat had managed to rope his heart with her easy acceptance of who he was and what he wanted out of a woman. She hadn't yet accepted she was theirs, lock stock and barrel, but she would.

Chapter Eight

Sawyer was in the kitchen frying bacon when Rachel emerged from Rogan's bedroom the next morning. He had spent most of the night wishing it was him in her bed and not his brothers. It was ridiculous to be so smitten with a woman who resisted a commitment, but it was his reality right now.

She nearly brought him to his knees when she stepped into the kitchen, freshly showered and dressed in a pair of well-worn blue jeans, a t-shirt advertising the local rodeo, and bare feet. Even her toes were sexy, how was that even possible?

"Morning, Sawyer. Mmm…something smells good in here," she spoke from across the room, and her body language gave her away. Her nerves were back and she was worried about what they would think of her in the morning light.

Beckoning her with his free hand, he was pleased when she walked directly to his side. "Morning, baby. Did you sleep well?" He wrapped his arm around her, pulling her in against his chest, and pressing his nose against her still damp hair.

"Better than I expected. I'm not so sure about Parker and Rogan though. Rogan hit the floor at least once last night. Parker was lucky enough to have the side of the bed that was close to the wall." They both laughed, and Sawyer squeezed her tighter.

"Tonight Hudson and I are taking our chances with you. I'll be damned if I'll have you for a weekend and not have the pleasure of sleeping next to you."

She giggled, "Alright, but it's your funeral. So whatcha making?"

"Bacon and pancakes. Sound good?" The moan of pleasure she let out had his cock hardening in his jeans and he shifted her so she was pinned between him and the counter top. "Mmm, I'll take that as a yes. Want a taste?"

He dipped his finger in the sticky syrup sitting nearby, and then lifted it to her lips. Watching in amazement as those plump, pink lips parted for him and sucked deeply at his appendage. His cock throbbed against his zipper, and he pressed it firmly into her belly as her tongue danced over the tip of his finger. She released him with a loud "pop" and grinned up at him.

"Tastes decadent, but you know, I'm not really a bacon kinda girl."

For just a moment Sawyer frowned down at the little brunette bundle, thinking he had actually made a mistake in selecting breakfast, but the wicked grin that split her face had his curiosity peaked. "Not a bacon lover? What kind of red-blooded Texas girl are you?"

"I'm actually more of a sausage fan…" her hand slid to the zipper that was already stretched to its capacity over his erection, and he sucked in a breath through his teeth when she squeezed his shaft.

"Fuck, Rachel!"

"Shut off the stove, Sawyer. We can eat later."

He didn't even hesitate as he flipped the burner off, feeling no remorse for the pancake, which remained on the griddle and would be wasted. If his woman was horny, he was damn sure going to oblige her in some morning fun, especially if it meant he got her all to himself.

Handing her the bottle of syrup, he scooped her up in his arms and whisked her into the office just off the kitchen. It was the closest room with a locking door, and he was determined to make use of its privacy. Kicking the door closed behind him, he sat her down on the edge of the large cherry wood desk, and quickly pushed the few items covering it to the floor. With one step he had the door locked and he was back in Rachel's arms. Lips locked and teeth clashing as they both reached for the ecstasy they could only achieve together.

He tugged her shirt up over her head and dropped it to the floor, pleased to find her bra-less and arching up into his touch. Clamping his lips over one nipple, he suckled hard drawing a yelp and a hiss of breath from her.

"Oh my God, Sawyer!"

She leaned back to rest on her elbows, and he quickly pulled her jeans down her thighs. When he pulled them off her ankles, he took a moment to bend and press a kiss to the arch of each of her sexy bare feet. Her moan of pleasure had him kissing his way up to the glorious V between her thighs.

Her scent was a seductive blend of wild flowers and woman, arousal and springtime. The power of his own need to claim her took his breath away. Feeling like a sap, he tugged her flimsy satin panties to one side and pressed a hot opened mouth kiss to her pussy. She was already wet, and her juices were sweet and tangy.

"Oh my God, Sawyer!" she whimpered, and wiggled underneath his feasting mouth.

Pausing, Sawyer snagged the bottle of syrup from where it had landed next to her hip, and drizzled the sticky sweetness over the dip of her belly between her hips, and in a line down to her sweet spot. She shivered with anticipation, and he nearly dropped the bottle on her.

"What are you doing now, cowboy?" she asked with a giggle.

"Well, ma'am, my breakfast was rudely interrupted, so I'm going to eat out." He didn't need to wait for her response. He knew she was just as turned on as he was. There was a light pink flush covering her cheeks, throat, and upper chest, and her lips were parted with her heavy breathing.

The sweet sugar of the syrup paired with the delicious fragrance of Rachel made his knees buckle, and he knelt between her spread thighs lapping up the syrup and her cream furiously. She began to thrust against him, and her fingernails found his scalp. Scoring the skin and tugging at his hair, encouraging him to continue and begging him to stop all at once. Taking in every subtle thrust and arch of her hips, he followed her with his tongue, pressing into her warm cavity before flickering over her pulsing clit.

"Sweet Jesus! Sawyer, let me come!"

"You got it, sexy," he said it just loud enough for her to hear him over her pants, and then he pressed two fingers into her pussy while sucking her clit between his lips. She shattered underneath him, crying out and shivering with passion. Moisture flooded out of her cunt and over his fingers, and he lapped it up with joy. Bringing her pleasure was more satisfying than any orgasm he could remember having, like a drug, he craved more of it.

Her fingers found his hair and she tugged at him until he rose up over her limp body. "Yes, ma'am?"

"That….was…amazing."

Pride filled his chest, and his cock twitched in response. "You're welcome."

She giggled, "I hope you aren't ready to call it quits just yet. You know, usually when I partake in a meal I get filled up, and I haven't felt very full yet."

Sawyer reached down to release his cock from his jeans while he pressed another kiss to her mouth, "Don't worry, baby, I will fill you up again and again until you're completely satisfied."

He retrieved a condom from the back pocket of his jeans, and slid it on over his aching dick. Taking his cock in hand, he ran it up and down her pussy lips. The little wriggle and whimper she gave were hypnotic, and he couldn't drag his eyes away from the sight of his cock stretching her puffy pussy lips apart. Easing into her, he savored the scorching hot sensation of her body, and the lusty groan that rumbled out of her throat.

When his balls hit her ass cheeks, he sighed with pleasure and wrapped his hands around her hipbones to hold her in place. "Are you full yet, Rachel?"

"Completely," she moaned and rolled her hips up to him, making his jaw clench and his balls tighten.

"Good, now hold on, baby."

He began to thrust his cock in and out of her tight pussy, tipping her hips so he pressed against her G-spot every time he sunk into her. Listening to her whimper, moan, and cry out her pleasure as he brought her back to the edge of orgasm.

"Sawyer, please!"

"Yes, baby, come for me, Rachel, come all over my cock."

Her body reacted to his demand and she arched violently up off the desk. Her fingers dug into the muscles of his biceps, and her ankles locked behind him with her heels resting on his ass. There was no way she could have known how comforting her hold was, or how much he needed to feel the bite of her fingernails in his skin. She couldn't possibly know how important it was to him to have those love marks on him to prove this wasn't a dream.

Rachel's cunt convulsed around him, and he stopped fighting his own orgasm, filling the condom and dropping his weight onto his elbows at her sides. It was a good fifteen minutes before either took the initiative to pull away and clean up. There was only one pancake casualty, and the bacon was perfectly cooked if slightly cold. All in all it was the best morning Sawyer had ever experienced, and he was praying that it was the first one in a lifetime of perfect mornings with Rachel.

****

Rogan's voice interrupted Rachel and Sawyer's playful banter over the breakfast dishes. "Someone looks like the cat that ate the parakeet this morning."

"I do believe it's the canary, bro, but I did eat well this morning. In fact, I feasted on the sweetest delicacy—"

Sawyer's sexy innuendo was cut off when Rachel planted her elbow under his rib cage. "Hush! Yes, you could say I'm in a good mood this morning. I spent all of last night having wickedly hot sex with four delicious brothers, why wouldn't I be smiling?"

Rogan moved closer and pressed a tender kiss on Rachel's still puffy lips. When he lifted his head, she couldn't tear her gaze away from the dark desire in his eyes. "I have to admit, sexual satisfaction looks good on you, love."

Pleasure filled her chest, and she rose up on her toes to kiss him again. This time there was no tenderness, only passion and possession as his tongue forced its way past her lips and stroked over her teeth. It took everything she had to break the kiss and step backwards so her lungs could refill with badly needed oxygen.

"Wanna go for a ride, cowgirl?"

A red-hot blush crept over her cheeks, and she glanced over her shoulder at Sawyer who nodded. "Go on. Make him take you all over our property on a tour. Wear him out and maybe he won't be so obnoxious later."

"Well if that's not reason enough…" Rogan looked at her hopefully, and she laughed.

"I'd love to go riding, and I would love a tour of the ranch. Let me get my boots." She spun around on her heels and headed for the doorway humming the Big and Rich country song "Save a Horse, Ride a Cowboy" as she went, and their joint laughter filled her ears.

****

"I have to admit, I don't think I've ever seen a more beautiful spot in my life." Rachel and Rogan sat atop their horses at the edge of a crest looking down at the pond that separated Brooks Pastures from the Raft Ranch. The oblong body of water was about the length of two football fields and a third of that wide. Trees lined the edges of it except for one end where a fishing dock had been built and a fire pit had been dug into the bank.

"This is probably my favorite place in the world. I like to come down here and think." Rogan dismounted from his horse, and walked to her side to help her down as well. Tugging her back against his chest, he turned her and pointed. "See that tree right on the curve there, the one with the giant rock near the trunk? That one has an old rope swing in it that my brothers and I convinced our dad to hang when we were in junior high. We would spend hours down here fishing, swimming, camping, and just being kids."

"It sounds like the ideal childhood."

"Yeah, I suppose it was. We were lucky to have parents who loved each other deeply, and loved us even more. Someday I want to share that same love with my wife and children," Rogan spoke softly, but he felt her body stiffen at his words. Knowing he was skimming the surface of a sensitive subject, he patiently waited for her response.

"I hope you are able to fulfill that dream. Your family will be lucky to have you." The words were tender, and he heard the tension in them, as though she had to force them out of her throat.

"Tell me about your family, Rachel. I only know the town rumors, and we all know how often those are right."

She turned in his arms, and gave him a half smile while staring up into his eyes, "I'm not sure you're ready for all of that…chaos. Let's walk down to the bank. Did you know I was a champion rock skipper as a kid? No one could beat me."

Rogan desperately wanted to argue, but the sway of her hips as she made her way down the steep embankment fogged his brain. Wasn't that why he brought her here in the first place? To have a wonderful "time out" with her, and a quiet point to talk, away from all of his brothers. A chance to make love to her without anyone else interrupting them. On that thought he followed her, grinning at her pleasure as she began to collect flat rocks.

"The trick is to find the right rock. It has to be flat and smooth, but not too big or it will be too heavy to bounce." She spun and a rock sprung out of her hand bouncing several times across the glassy surface of the pond. The delighted laugh that bubbled out of her throat filled an empty spot in Rogan's soul.

"I wouldn't have taken you for a rock skipping champ. Hudson was always the best at this game, just like I was always the best student, Parker was the heavy lifter and the athlete, and Sawyer was the funniest. We each had our talents."

She flashed him a smoldering smile, "Oh, I've already figured that out. You four are very talented men."

Suddenly the sensitive sweet side of Rogan disappeared as all of the blood pooled in his balls and his cock slammed against his zipper. "No, love, you haven't even begun to scratch the surface of our hidden "talents" yet."

"Really? I mean, I would have thought you would have given me your best game on the first shot, just to make sure you got a second chance…"

His eyes narrowed at the challenge, and he stepped menacingly toward her. Stalking her as though she was prey. "You weren't impressed? I seem to recall a lot of screaming for an unimpressive event."

"I didn't say I wasn't impressed. I just said I was disappointed you were holding back on me. What other little secrets are you keeping bottled up inside of you, Rogan?"

Just like that, he had her pressed against the wide trunk of a Maple tree, her legs spread on either side of his and her mouth parting underneath the onslaught of his kiss. He devoured her, savoring her flavor, branding the feel of her skin under his fingertips into his brain.

Sliding one hand down to cup her ass, he threaded the other hand into her thick hair and held her in place so he could make love to her mouth. Their hips rocked together in a motion as old as time, and as seductive as a siren's call. He couldn't bear the thought of being separated from her any longer, and he pulled back so he could release the button on her jeans, and she tugged at his zipper.

"Hurry, Rogan! I want you!"

The roaring in his ears grew louder at her plea, and he groaned, "Fuck. That's all I needed to hear, baby."

It took another minute to get her boots and jeans off, but he didn't pause to finish stripping her. Slipping a condom over his already aching cock, he lifted her until she locked her ankles around his lean hips lining her pussy up with him. Placing one hand between her back and the rough bark of the tree, he used the other to guide and steady her hips as he sunk into her warmth.

Like adding kindling to a fire, he went up in smoke the moment his cock hit her cervix. The feeling of completion was intense, and he had to close his eyes to keep from telling her how much it meant to him. She reached out to him, gripping his shoulders, and pressing her breasts into his chest as she buried her face in his neck. Her moans echoed his thrusts as he took her fast and hard, not even flinching when she bit into his shoulder and climaxed in a magnificent display of sexual satisfaction.

Again and again he pumped his cock into her, refusing to allow himself to come because it would end the pleasure. Her whimper of pain froze him mid-thrust, and he jerked his head back to stare down into her face in horror.

"What is it, love? Did I hurt you?"

She grimaced before giving him a small smile, "The tree—"

Even with his hand between her shoulder blades and the tree, his enthusiasm had drilled her lower body into the bark. When he withdrew from her and turned her around, he could see the raw red skin where it scraped her.

"Holy hell! I'm so sorry, Rach." He reached for his zipper, but she stopped him by wrapping her hand around his latex covered cock.

"Don't! I don't want you to stop, but we should probably find a more suitable location." Relief rushed from his brain to his balls at her words and he cast a quick glance at the surrounding landscape looking for a spot that would be easier on her. A frown puckered his brow as he considered and dismissed several locations before she spoke again.

"Really? It doesn't have to be so complicated Rogan. Come on!" He couldn't keep from laughing as she tugged her shirt off and then put her boots on her bare feet and meandered closer to the pond naked. His laughter quickly gave way to raw lust while he watched her sweet ass sway back and forth like pond grass. She walked all the way to the end of the dock before she stopped and shucked her boots off. "What's taking you so long? Don't you want me anymore?"

"Believe me, Rachel, watching you walk through the trees and grass naked has me harder than a fence post. Now I'm just waiting to see what you do next."

She flashed him a seductive grin, before doing a cannon ball off the end of the dock into the water. Pleasure filled him, and maybe even a little pride. This woman was unlike anyone he had ever been with. She was proud and driven, with a witty intelligence that kept him on his toes but then, she would do something so off the wall like jump into a pond naked, knocking him to his knees. She rose up nearly silently from the water like a sea nymph, water running down her face, and her brown hair slicked back on her head. Those wide dark brown eyes met his, and she wiggled her finger in invitation.

"Come on in, Rogan, the water's warm."

He didn't hesitate any longer, stripping his clothes off while he walked toward the sexiest woman alive. Dropping apparel here and there, he managed to be down to his skin by the time he reached the edge of the dock. Taking a page out of her book, he cannonballed into the water next to her knowing it would splash her, and hoping when he rose up she wouldn't be pissed.

The smile on Rachel's face was electrifying as he inhaled fresh air and made his way to her side. Without a word, he pulled her against him and she instinctively wrapped her legs around his hips. Kicking off with his lower body, he swam them closer to the bank, not stopping until his feet hit the sandy bottom. Here was perfect. Here he had a stable base so he could gain momentum and rock this woman's world.

She was one step ahead of him, capturing his mouth in a desperate kiss that drew his balls up tight. Her thigh muscles were stronger than he expected and he groaned deeply when she lifted up and sank down onto his hard cock. They were united. Two pieces of one whole, meshed together in the water, writhing against each other in passion. It was mind-blowing.

Using one hand to brace her neck so she couldn't pull away from his mouth, he used the other to guide her hips in his preferred rhythm, and then he made love to her. With every touch, stroke, and lick, they climbed higher up the mountain of desire. He didn't release her lips until she started to tremble in his arms, and when he did, he was rewarded with a loud moan and his own name in her sweet, sexy voice.

"Come for me, love. Give it to me!" He thrust into her while pulling her hips down at the same time, giving them both the ultimate contact possible, and she exploded around him. Her scream carried on the wind, and his yell echoed behind it. Cum shot out of him, heating them both, and making her pussy much more slippery. Slippery. That word—that thought—brought him around like ice water on a flame.

"Oh fuck! Rachel, honey, don't freak out okay. The condom is gone."

"The condom is gone."

****

The condom? What?

It took a couple of seconds for Rachel to process Rogan's words, but when they settled, they were a heavy weight in her heart.

"You're joking, right," she whispered, staring into his worried eyes.

"Rach, I'm sorry! It must have slipped off when I jumped in, and I was just too focused on you to realize it." Rogan really looked miserable. His brown eyes were wide and nervous, and his hands clutched at her hips in a death grip. Every muscle in his body was taut with anxiety as he waited for her reaction.

She wasn't sure what her reaction should be. It was an accident, not something done deliberately, yet it could cause detrimental consequences for both of them. Her stomach twisted as she imagined being pregnant with Rogan's baby. A miracle and a tragedy all in one blow. The knowledge she was on birth control soothed her but didn't completely eliminate the fear.

This was only temporary. One weekend. Forty-eight hours of hot, dirty sex with four brothers and then everyone went their separate ways…so why did her heart suddenly hurt at the thought of leaving tomorrow? She didn't doubt for a second that Rogan would be a great dad, and would want a part in his child's life, but how would his three brothers feel?

"I'm on birth control. I'm sure we're alright. No more accidents though, m'kay?" She forced a smile to her lips as he sighed with relief.

"Thank God. I promise, it won't happen again, love."

Rachel knew he intended his words to sound comforting, but instead they burned in her chest. Did he have to sound so relieved? Clearly she needed to keep the temporary status of this relationship front and center in her brain because Rogan was not interested in permanence. The idea of her getting pregnant nearly sent him into an apoplectic fit. No, it was for the best that she have her fun now and then pack her bags tomorrow and leave the Brooks brothers behind.

"Let's head back to the house, your brothers are probably wondering what happened to us." She gave him a fleeting kiss before she disengaged herself from his body and made her way onto the bank.

There was nothing to dry off on, so she forced her clothes on over her wet skin, grimacing as her jeans chaffed against the raw scrape on her lower back. As erotic as it was to be taken against a tree, she now felt the fantasy was grossly exaggerated. She would likely have a bruise there for weeks. A black and blue reminder of what was, and what could never be.

Rogan climbed out of the pond beside her and began to dress. When they were both put back together, he grabbed her hand and brought it to his lips. "Thank you, love. That was one of the most memorable moments of my life."

She giggled at his gallantry, "The look on your face when I jumped in the water was priceless. Now, let's go. I didn't realize we had been out here so long, but my stomach is growling."

Rogan studied her face for a moment, looking like he had something he wanted to say, but instead he tucked her hand in his large one and led her back up to the horses. He silently helped her mount hers, leaving her with a soft pat on her round ass before gracefully mounting his own. Rachel turned her horse to follow him, allowing herself one more quick look at the pond, hoping the memory of the moment would be burned into her brain forever. It would be something to look back on and remember how wonderful it was to just let go of everything for a few minutes, and enjoy spending time with someone who wanted her around.

Shutting out all of her regretful mental meanderings, she followed Rogan back up the slope and in the general direction of the ranch house. Knowing three other men awaited her attention there made her heart skip a beat, and her tongue go dry. She couldn't remember why she agreed to this in the first place, but she was sure as hell glad she did.

Chapter Nine

It didn't take them long to reach the ranch house, and Rachel hurried to change into a pair of shorts instead of her damp blue jeans. The last thing she needed was more chafed skin when she still had twenty-four hours of horny men ahead of her.

By the time she reentered the kitchen, Rogan had scrounged up sandwich fixings and was already digging into a plate of food.

He glanced up at her with a guilty smile, "Umm... help yourself."

"I see you wait like a hog at a trough," she said with a giggle.

"Sorry, I was really hungry. I promise I'll be a perfectly polite gentleman later."

She leaned forward and licked a dab of mustard off the corner of his mouth before whispering, "I prefer you when you're not being polite, and I avoid gentlemen."

Lust speared through her as she watched his eyes darken and his jaw clench, but before he could respond Hudson walked in the kitchen door. He froze as he surveyed the scene and then let out a low wolf's whistle. "Damn, you two could melt an igloo with the heat coming off you. What did I miss? Catch me up so I can play too."

Rachel let out a loud laugh, and accepted the hug and kiss Hudson offered as he reached her side. "Rogan took me out skinny dippin', and now he's feeding me so I don't wither away after burning so many calories last night with you fine *gentlemen*."

She winked at Rogan as she enunciated the word, and he grinned back.

"Ah yes, we must make sure to keep your energy levels up. We don't want you wimping out on us before the end of our contract," Hudson said with a serious look on his face.

"Wimping out? If I didn't know you were joking, funny man, I would hurt you for that comment," she said flippantly, throwing a potato chip at him. When he caught it in his mouth and shot her a wicked grin, she stuck her tongue out at him.

"Honey, do your worst. I promise I'll love it."

"On that note I have to leave you two. I have some work I need to get done this afternoon. Hudson, Mack said that there is a fence down on the North ridge, can you make a run up there and check it out before dinner?"

"Yep, maybe I'll take Rach out with me." Rogan disappeared into the office shutting the door behind him, and Hudson shot her a questioning glance to which she shook her head in the negative.

"Uh uh. This cowgirl needs to rest her weary ass and stay off a saddle for a few days. Wet denim isn't good for soft skin, and it's been years since I rode regularly." She stood to put her plate in the sink, and Hudson snagged her arm tugging her into his lap.

"Rode hard and put up satisfied, right, Rach?"

She couldn't stop the laugh that tumbled out of her, or the feeling of comfort and contentment she got when one of her men was holding her. Her men. That's how she was beginning to think of them. What a scary thought. If they knew she was starting to have feelings for them, how would they respond?

Ice cold fear filled her belly, and she pushed away from Hudson, shutting that line of thoughts down quickly.

"Something like that I suppose. Where are Sawyer and Parker by the way?" The distinct wobble to her voice belied her airy question, but she refused to meet Hudson's questioning gaze, focusing instead on clearing away the dishes from her own meal.

"Parker is in the barn, and Sawyer…um…honestly, I'm not sure where he wandered off to. Hey, Rachel, are you okay? Did I say something wrong there?" She turned away from the dishwasher and ran into his broad chest, letting out a squeak of surprise.

"Oh, sorry, Hudson. No nothing is wrong. I think I'm just antsy. I don't sit still very well."

He stared down at her with a curious frown marring his beautifully chiseled face, and for a moment she thought he would argue with her, but he didn't. He just pressed a kiss to her lips, stealing her breath and leaving her week-kneed, before he lifted his head and smiled. "Alright, I'm going to head on out but when I get back this evening, you and I are going to take a bubble bath I think. A good hot soaking and a massage will ease those aching muscles."

She sighed and let her eyes roll skyward, "That sounds heavenly. You've got a date, cowboy."

Hudson gave her another brief kiss then headed back out the door leaving her alone in their kitchen trying to keep her emotions under control. When she agreed to this last night, she had no idea what a veritable rollercoaster of feelings she would be jumping on. From one moment to the next she wasn't sure if she wanted to walk away from them, or if she wanted to fall to her knees and ask them to keep her. This was truly not her brightest moment. She should have walked away last night.

Like a movie, the events of the last twenty-four hours rolled through her mind. Every single explosively hot orgasm tightened her stomach and made her pussy clench. No, she wouldn't go back and change her decision. If nothing else, she would have those memories to fantasize about for the rest of her life. She knew there was no future here. Four men and one woman was not a stable relationship. All of her life she had watched her mother struggle with a broken heart, and if she bared her soul to the four brothers, she knew she would find herself nursing an emotional wound too. It just wasn't worth it.

Gaining her control back, she decided the best way to keep her mind off the future, was to focus on the present. A smile graced her face as she prepared a couple of sandwiches and headed off toward the barn in search of Parker.

****

Parker had just finished spreading hay in one of the stalls when Rachel sauntered into the barn looking sexy as hell. Short denim shorts that rivaled anything Daisy Duke ever wore showcased her long, slim legs that ended in tiny bare feet with sexy pale pink toenails. The afternoon sunlight caught her brown hair making it glow a copper color, and her big brown doe eyes looked a little apprehensive as she looked around the barn.

"It must be my lucky day," he said as he leaned the pitchfork against the wall and began removing his leather gloves. He waited for her to come to him, pleased when she did so as soon as she spotted him.

"I figured you probably hadn't had anything for lunch yet, and Rogan, Hudson, and I just had sandwiches." She held a plate out to him with two sandwiches on it, both neatly made and cut in half diagonally. For some reason the little extra effort sucker punched him in the gut. How many years had it been since a woman cared enough about him to make him lunch? When he tore his gaze away from the tiny triangular sandwiches, he found her staring at him with an odd expression. "Well?"

Embarrassment flooded through him, "I'm sorry, what did you ask?"

Her lips turned down in dismay, and she suddenly looked very uncomfortable. "I just asked if you could take a break, but if you're busy it's no big deal. I could use a nap, so…yeah…maybe I should just go back inside—"

She started to turn away from him, but he reached out and grabbed her hand, stopping her words and her motion. "Wait, don't go. I will gladly make time for a break as long as you promise to sit with me while I eat."

The smile of pleasure that graced her beautiful face was nearly enough to unman him, and he swallowed back a groan.

"Sure."

He led her out the doors of the barn and over to several bales of hay that were stacked near the corral. She barely glanced at the seat he gestured to, and he watched in surprised fascination as she took several steps closer so she could lean on the fence and watch his horse in the enclosure.

"Did you enjoy your ride this morning, sunshine?"

She gave him a confused look before nodding, "You mean with Rogan? Yes, I had a great time. He took me out to the pond, and I taught him how to skip rocks."

Parker laughed loudly. That was what he loved about Rachel Morgan. She found the fun in everything she did. "Good, you'll have to grant me the privilege of taking you out on the trail sometime. The Carrion River is only about a day's hard ride from here, and there are several good camping sites around there."

A wistful expression drifted across her features and she pursed her lips as though deep in thought. She didn't even acknowledge his words, and it stung. He bit into a sandwich and forced himself to chew. It was probably a great sandwich, but at the moment it tasted like sawdust. His normally take charge attitude was suffering a major setback and the blame lay solely at her feet. When she was around he couldn't seem to focus on anything, but her. The idea that she wasn't feeling the same way was painfully sharp in his brain.

"What's his name?" she asked as she watched the stallion graze in the field.

"Romeo."

She laughed and it rippled through him teasing at the need in his gut. "Really? Where is Juliet?"

"Pregnant in the other barn. She should foal anytime, so she can't be with her lover."

Rachel's eyes lit up as she finally turned and faced him. "That seems rather unfair. To take two star crossed lovers and keep them apart when she's obviously facing something so monumental."

He couldn't resist rolling his eyes. "Yeah...well, I have a pretty good feeling they will be back together soon enough. Besides, Romeo here is quite the ladies' man. Juliet is the third mare he's knocked up this year."

"Really? Wow! Impressive odds. Guess Juliet probably learned her lesson. The pretty ones are always the playboys." She looked up at him through her eyes lashes with a teasing smile, but he couldn't help but think there was more to her statement than just a joke.

They sat watching the big black stallion as he slowly moved around the corral, and Parker hurried to eat the rest of his meal. When he swallowed the last bite and put the plate down on the hay bale, he looked up to find her watching him instead. A wave of apprehension went through him. This was the first time he had been alone with her, and all he wanted was to strip her clothes off and claim her in every physical and emotional way, but it was more important they talk. He had questions he needed answered.

"Do you want a quick tour of the horse barn?"

Her eyes lit up, and she nodded, "That would be great!"

They headed across the yard to the main horse barn where most of their pregnant mares were housed. He reached out and took her hand as they walked, lacing their fingers together when she didn't resist.

"I'm glad you came with us this weekend, Rachel," he said softly, and she turned surprised eyes up to him. A warmth filled the chocolate pools as she smiled back.

"Me too. I haven't had this much fun in years."

"You could stay longer, you know. You don't have to leave tomorrow." His breath caught in his chest at her silence, and he felt her pull away from him. Emotionally she was bruised, maybe scarred, and he wasn't sure how to overcome her fears just yet. Choosing to let the subject drop, he started to talk as they walked through the barn. "This is Freckles here, and she is having her first foal, and next to her is Magic. Doc is pretty sure she is having twins this time. The gray one there is Ghost Dancer, she's new to the ranch, and she isn't pregnant, but she's awfully skittish. She's a rescue horse, so we have a ways to go before she's comfortable here. We're taking our time getting to know each other right now."

"A rescue horse?" Rachel moved very slowly to the door of the stall where Ghost Dancer was moving restlessly.

"Yeah, I don't know the whole story but the way I understand it, she was found nearly starved to death and badly injured from whipping sores that hadn't been treated and hadn't healed. A few more days, maybe a week, and she would have died. Sawyer can probably give you more details. He was the one that went and got her when the agency called. I couldn't leave that weekend."

She watched him closely, and he reached out to brush her dark hair away from her cheek. "So you're telling me that Mr. Parker Brooks, badass cowboy, has a soft spot for abused and injured animals?"

He shrugged in response, and she giggled, stepping closer to him.

"Well, Mr. Brooks, just so you know, I find that to be a very sexy quality in a man."

That got his attention. His cock throbbed behind his zipper, coming to life in a painfully obvious way, and he groaned when she pressed a little kiss to the bottom of his jaw. "You're playing with fire, sunshine."

"Yeah, so maybe I'll get a little burned. It is awfully hot in here." She reached for his zipper and he stopped her with his lightning fast reflexes. "Hey! What's the problem?"

"Rachel, there are things about me you don't understand yet."

"Really? So fill me in. Tell me something that would surprise me." Her chin tilted up defiantly and she stepped back crossing her arms over her chest. The stance was pure brat, and he wanted to bend her over his knee and spank her ass red for challenging him, but that would be too much too fast. If he wanted to keep her, he needed to proceed with caution.

"I want kids."

She stared at him in shock as her jaw fell open. "What?"

"You said, 'tell me something that would surprise me,' so I did. I want kids. I love kids, and I'm hoping when I settle down to have a half a dozen of them." His gut tightened waiting for her reaction. He had left off the part about wanting kids with her, but being the first time he had ever admitted his desire for children out loud, he figured he could be forgiven for the omission.

"Wow. Okay, yeah, you surprised me. I think you'd make a great dad. All four of you guys will make good dads someday." She turned and faced the horse in the stall in front of her, attempting to put distance between them again.

When he stayed in place and waited silently, she fidgeted, and moved on to the next stall. "Who is this?"

"Cashmere. She is actually Hudson's horse, but he wanted to try breeding her. This is her first foal too."

The silence grew and he could almost hear her brain spinning. She was deep in thought as she stared at the solid black mare in the stall.

"My dad bailed on my mom when I was young. He fell in love with his secretary, and they had an affair. In a matter of moments one Sunday evening over dinner, my life went from perfectly happy to a complete wreck. They moved to Seattle to be close to her family when the divorce was final, and she got pregnant. He has a whole new family there, and has completely forgotten about the daughter he left in Texas."

Parker's heart broke for her, but he remained quiet, afraid if he spoke up now she would stop talking. Cashmere moved closer to Rachel so she could stroke her hand over her face, and Parker tried not to fall to his knees. Rachel was everything to him at this point. Years of watching and wanting her had taken their toll on his life. Sure, he had been with other women, but none of them meant as much to him as this little spitfire did after only twenty-four hours in his home. Several minutes passed before she spoke again.

"You know, Mitch had a lot to say about my dysfunctional family, but then again compared to his perfect life, mine seemed pretty fucked up."

"Don't curse." The words slipped out of his mouth instinctively and he saw her stiffen at his demand. Damn it. He couldn't change his nature. This was who he was, and if she couldn't tolerate it, he should know it sooner rather than later.

"I'm sorry. Talking about Mitch just brings out the worst in me." Her words eased an odd pressure that had been building in his chest, and he finally moved to her side reaching out to wrap his arms around her waist and draw her back against his chest.

"What happened with Mitch, Rach?"

"Ah you know the story, small town white trash girl from a broken family hooks up with the son of a political giant in said small town, only to be raked across the coals when he realizes he can do better."

Her snarky tone sent his blood pressure sky rocketing, and he felt himself squeezing her a little tighter. "Cut the bitchy attitude. You and I both know Mitch could never do better than you, and if he thinks that Connie is better...well then he's just a special kind of stupid."

She laughed, and relaxed a little in his arms. "I have a bad habit of picking the wrong man."

"Maybe it's because you're only allowing yourself to pick one man." He knew he was pushing her, but he couldn't resist the opening.

"Or maybe I'm just not meant to be in a relationship." She turned in his arms and rose on her tiptoes to press a soft kiss to his lips. "I'm going to go back in the house and take a nap. Thanks for showing me the barn."

Parker wanted to argue. Every fiber of his being was telling him to keep her there and make her keep talking, but he knew in his heart that if she wanted to be with the four of them, eventually she would make the decision on her own. He couldn't force it. Nodding, he smiled back, "Thanks for lunch, sunshine. You make on hell of a bologna sandwich."

"It's so nice to be recognized for my many talents," she said playfully as she sauntered out of the barn, leaving Parker chuckling and Cashmere staring after her forlornly.

Parker reached out and stroked the soft hair on the horse's nose, "Yeah, she's pretty amazing isn't she? With any luck she'll let us keep her."

Chapter Ten

"You're joking right?" Parker looked really pissed.

"It wasn't like it was on purpose. It was an accident. I was in the moment, and I lost my head," Rogan said. His brown eyes narrowed in irritation as he faced off with two of his three brothers and explained that he had had sex with Rachel without a condom.

Sawyer threw his hands up, "Dude! Don't you think we all lose our minds when we're with her? You can't make that kind of mistake!"

"I know that, Sawyer. Look, she said she's on birth control, and I don't think she was upset about it." He ran his hand through his hair and plopped down on the couch heavily. Rachel and Hudson were currently in Parker's bathroom taking a bubble bath in the largest tub in the house. That was Hudson's way, he was a romantic at heart. All four brothers had just gotten back into the house when she came stumbling into the kitchen looking sleepy and tousled. Rachel didn't look too distraught when she linked hands with Hudson and disappeared down the hallway, in fact she looked downright excited about the impending pampering.

Rogan couldn't keep his mind focused while he worked all afternoon. The mental image of her pregnant with his child did crazy things to his brain and body, so he kept having to force his mind away from it. The odds of her getting pregnant from that one incident were very slim with her on birth control, but he couldn't keep from hoping just a little bit that it would happen. If she got pregnant then maybe she would reconsider the temporary status of their relationship. She didn't seem like the type to cut and run, and her heart was too big to shut her child's father out of its life.

"If she's pregnant we're moving her in," Parker said resolutely, and Sawyer barked out a laugh.

"Yeah? You and what army? Rachel doesn't exactly follow orders well, brother."

Sawyer was right, but Parker's Mr. Badass gene was probably going to try to prove he could force her. Rogan turned to Parker, "Sawyer's right, Parker, we can't make her do anything. I can't say I'm completely sorry it happened. I've only fucked one other woman bareback and that was Theresa McCray my freshman year of high school when I lost my virginity. Being with Rachel was…I don't know how to describe it. It was just magic."

"Okay, Casanova, but you might have just screwed this whole thing up for all of us. She's going to feel forced into a relationship if she's pregnant. We all agreed to seduce her this weekend, and then let the decision be hers." Sawyer rested his elbows on the kitchen table and chewed his lip. It was his tell, the only physical manifestation of his anxiety when something had him worried.

"I can't change it now! What's done is done," Rogan responded sharply. Anger and frustration were tinged with just a shade of shame in his gut.

"Yeah, we can't change it, but if she's pregnant it won't just be you tied up in it. It's just another good reason not to let her go tomorrow," Parker said, and Rogan rolled his eyes.

"You're such a douche, Parker. What woman wants to be treated like that? Like she doesn't have a mind of her own? Do you think Rachel can't make up her own mind about us?"

Parker stared back at Rogan silently, but his eyes looked shaken. In Parker's world everything was black and white. When something happened you made the choice you knew was right, and then went on with your life. Unfortunately he was almost too set in his desire to dominate, and Rogan was afraid he would scare Rachel off. He had seen her react submissively to Parker already, but the whole thing was still a novelty. How would she react to it on a day-to-day basis?

"Rogan is right, Parker, you need to ease up," Sawyer said.

"I know how to deal with Rachel, thank you very much. She and I had an interesting heart to heart in the barn earlier."

Rogan's ears perked up and he turned to face Parker, "Really? What about?"

"Did you know her dad had an affair and left her mom for another woman? He has a whole different family now, and he hasn't even tried to keep in touch with Rachel."

"Shit. Another fucktard that hurt her. We should start a list, because some day we're going to have to kick these guys' asses," Sawyer grumbled.

"And she believes she wasn't good enough for Mitch. That's why she's pushing us all away from her. Damn it, she thinks we're going to hurt her," Parker said, slamming his hand down on the table.

Rogan leaned forward on his elbows. "So we have to prove to her we aren't going to betray her trust. I hate to say this, but it means letting her leave tomorrow if that's what she wants."

Parker glared back at him, while Sawyer looked a little green around the gills, but neither one argued. The truth sucked, but there it was. Rogan would do anything to keep Rachel with them, but if that wasn't what made her the happiest, then it wasn't going to make him happy.

"I'm going to take a shower. When they come out, why don't we pop some popcorn and watch a movie? Let's show her we can all four spend time with her without sex too." Rogan's eyes skipped back and forth between his two brothers waiting for them to respond.

Sawyer cracked a small smile, "Good idea! I'll go pick a movie, Parker can make the popcorn."

"Fuck," Parker grumbled, but he stood and headed for the kitchen cabinet looking for their mom's old air popper. It had been a long time since the four brothers made time to have a movie night, and reinstating their mother's favorite family pastime with Rachel seemed perfect. Just so long as they didn't fuck it up.

****

Steam wafted up off the water, making the bathroom seem slightly hazy, and seductively intimate. Rachel was braced against Hudson's broad chest with his arms crossed over her bare breasts, and his fingers laced through hers. She could feel his heart beating through her back, and the coarse hairs on his legs tickling her own. It was peaceful to be sitting in the huge jetted tub that occupied Parker's bathroom with the baby of the four brothers. Of the four of them, Hudson was by far the quietest about the whole weekend's events. He seemed content just to enjoy holding her in a tub of bubbles.

"It's so quiet in here. It's almost as if no one else exists," she murmured, sighing and then smiling as her heavy breath sent bubbles skittering across the surface of the water.

"No one else does exist when I'm with you, Rach."

She giggled, and twisted so she could see his face, "Oh stop it. I don't need flowery words, Hudson."

A frown marred his brow and his jaw ticked, "You might not need them, but you deserve them, Rach. I want you to know how good it feels to have you in my arms, that way later, when you're alone in your own bed, maybe you will dream about me holding you."

She turned back around quickly to avoid his eyes. His words were intimidating. She didn't want to hurt any of these guys, but softhearted, sweet Hudson was the most likely victim of the bunch. In her heart she knew she was already attached to these four guys. They intrigued her, seduced her, and made her feel more special than anyone she had ever met, but how long could that last? A few weeks, months, perhaps even a few years, but ultimately the fire and intimacy would fizzle out and instead of being hurt by one man, she would end up hurt by four.

Hudson didn't let her linger in silence long as he began speaking while resting his chin atop her head. "Do you know the first time I really noticed you were all grown up was at the fundraiser for Millie Creason's family?"

"You mean the bake sale to replace their roof after the tornado? Really?" She was perplexed as the memories of that day four years ago drifted back to her.

Millie was a longtime resident of the area who was widowed when her husband was in a tragic farming accident. The following summer a nasty storm had blown through town and taken the top part of her home off, leaving her and her three children without shelter temporarily. The whole town had banded together to collect money in various ways and then rebuilt the missing parts of the structure in a matter of weeks.

"Yeah but, honey, you were wearing a pair of lipstick tight jeans that day, and believe me, you had the sweetest buns there."

Rachel burst out into laughter. "Oh my God. You are such a cheese ball."

"It's not cheesy if it's the truth, and I would never lie to you." Hudson sounded slightly offended, and she turned around, rising up on her knees to face him. Her breasts lifted out of the water and his gorgeous dark eyes focused on them immediately.

"You wouldn't huh? Not even a little white lie?" she asked, purposely swaying toward him seductively. His tongue darted out to lick his lips and his breathing grew a little rougher.

"Nope."

"So what if I asked you if something made my butt look big?"

The astonished look he gave her at her question had her giggling. His eyebrow lifted and his mouth hung open. "You're joking, right? You're ass is perfect, honey. Every time I lay eyes on it all I can think about is getting my hands on it."

Her pussy pulsed at his erotic words, and she suddenly felt overheated. "What if I wanted you to put your hands on it, Hudson."

A grin spread over his handsome face, "All you have to do is ask."

Taking that as her cue, she leaned into him, dragging her nipples across the bubbles that dotted his hard chest, and stopping a fraction of a breath away from his lips.

"Please?"

The whispered word barely made it between her lips before Hudson captured them. Instead of the fierce power and nuclear meltdown she seemed to feel when Rogan or Parker took her, she was slowly seduced by Hudson into a puddle of lust. He caressed her lips with his own, changing the pressure and angle every other moment, and taunting her tongue with his.

When she felt like she was ready to burst, she pushed one hand up the back of his neck and dug it into the hair at the base of his head, clutching him to her so he would kiss her long and deep. Instead of pulling away, he cupped both of her breasts in his hands, and teased her nipples with his callused thumbs.

The burning fire that had started in her pussy a moment ago was skittering under her skin now, and she started to feel desperate. Pushing at his knee, which had been resting against the side of the tub, she waited for him to straighten both legs so she could straddle him. Positioned comfortably astride his thighs, she reached for his cock, while he continued to play with her tits. He seemed to know exactly how tight to squeeze them, and how hard to pinch her nipples without hurting her. Now with his dick in her hot little hands, she stroked up and down its length, squeezing him firmly and enjoying the way he thickened against her palms.

She liked having a little control over him, knowing he trusted her enough to let her have her way. He wasn't resisting her direction, he just continued his slow and steady seduction of her senses, keeping her slightly off balance by occasionally nipping her lip, or tugging at the length of her hair.

Rachel slid a hand down between his legs to cup his large balls, rolling them and enjoying the heavy weight of them. Wondering how much she could push him, she slid a finger toward the base of his sack then closer to his anus. His hiss of breath made her pause and look up at him, but his eyes were closed and his head was thrown back. He still had one hand cupping her breast, but the other was gripping the side of the huge tub as if he was trying to stay grounded in a flood. Encouraged, she ran her fingertip over the tiny pucker, grinning when it clenched under her touch.

Just how far would he let her go?

The tip of her finger pressed into the tight ring of muscles before it pushed her back out denying her entry. Determined and dazed with desire, she pressed forward, this time bending to lick the crown of his cock where it poked out of the water. His pelvis rocked upward, pushing his cock against her lips and relaxing his ass so her finger was able to breach it.

Hudson's moans of pleasure were making her brain fuzz over. Alternately licking and sucking the inch or so of cock she could reach above the water, she pushed her way deeper into his ass. When she reached the length of her finger, she curled it up finding that hot button she had always been curious about, and wriggling her finger against it.

Just like she had hoped his whole body clenched with pleasure, he hissed out her name, and let go of her breast to wrap his hand in her hand pulling tightly.

"Fuck! Enough! I'm going to come down your throat if you keep that up, Rach."

She grinned at him, feeling her chest swell with pride at the dark desire in his eyes. She had done that. Hudson desired her and no one else at this moment. It was a heady feeling, and it made her feel deliciously feminine.

He leaned forward, directing her to move backwards with his hand in her hair. Skillfully reining her with his creative lead, he had her turn around and bend over the side of the tub. With her upper chest braced against the tub rim, and her hands clenching the porcelain edge tightly, she told him what she wanted.

"Hudson, please fuck me. I need you!"

"With pleasure, honey." Completely submerged under the warm water, the bulbous head of his cock pressed against her slick opening finding an easy path into her depths. He was slow and deliberate in the way he fucked her, stirring a bonfire in her abdomen that went nuclear when he finally pinched her clit and sent her over the edge of reason.

They rested there panting in unison, his large frame draped over her much smaller one, sheltering and comforting her. The steam seemed to roll off them as the heat from the water paired with the heat of their bodies to create a fog-filled bathroom.

"You are the only person I would ever let do that, Rachel," he murmured into her ear, making her cunt clench around his still semi-hard cock.

"Mmm…I like the sound of that cowboy, and I definitely liked the end result." She giggled when he nipped her ear lobe, and shivered as the adrenaline drained out of her.

It was a few moments later when she felt his cum dribbling out of her into the water that she realized they hadn't used a condom. Once was understandable, but twice in one day was just asking for trouble.

"Hudson?"

"Yeah, honey?" He was still braced over her, with his lips brushing the top her spine and his nose buried in her hair.

"Umm…you didn't use a condom."

She felt him tense up behind her, and she waited for him to process it.

"Oh shit. I'm sorry, Rachel. I just didn't think about it. Are you pissed?" He moved backwards to sit on his heels as she turned to face him.

"I can't be mad at you. I didn't remember it either. I'm a little freaked out though."

He looked horrified, "Why? Rachel, if something happened—"

"No, you don't understand, Hudson. Earlier today, Rogan and I…well… we kind of had the same accident, which means that I've had unprotected sex with both of you in the same day. I'm on birth control, but if something when wrong I wouldn't know whose baby it was." Rachel's stomach twisted into a knot at the thought. This was a huge situation, and it was already too late to fix it. Her heart ached in her chest as she thought about how hurt Sawyer and Parker would be when they found out what she had let happen.

Hudson's worried expression melted into confusion as he stared at her, "So? Why would it matter?"

"Are you kidding me? Hudson, I just told you that if end up pregnant it may or may not be your brother's baby!"

He sat silently watching her with his head cocked to the side, and she got the distinct impression he could see into her soul. She only prayed that wasn't true, because she would die if he knew about the little thrill she got imagining herself carrying his or Rogan's child.

"You just don't get it do you, Rachel?"

"What?"

"Rachel, we don't care. We want you to be free with all four of us, and eventually we want you to carry a child for each of us. It would never matter whose baby you carried, because we would all claim it as our own. That's what being in a ménage relationship means, honey. It means we're one unit, not individual couples."

It settled in her ears, but took longer for her brain to absorb. He wasn't joking. They wanted a permanent ménage relationship with her. For just a brief moment her heart soared thinking that she could have it all. The four men she was falling in love with, and a half a dozen children to surround herself with so she would always be loved. But her own good sense quickly squashed that fantasy. There was no way that it would work like they wanted it to. How would she be able to keep up with four different relationships and try to blend them into one cohesive unit when she hadn't been able to make *one* relationship with *one* man work. Not to mention it wasn't exactly a legal sort of arrangement.

"You're forgetting one thing, Hudson," she said, taking a deep breath as she stood and stepped out of the tub, "we're not in a permanent relationship. We're having a weekend affair. Which means this could turn out to be the worst possible mistake we've ever made."

He was on his feet in front of her gripping her chin in his hand before she could stop him. "Or it could be the best thing to ever happen to us. Rachel, please, just give this a chance. Give us a chance. Stop shutting us out and let us show you that we can make it work."

"Really? So you're going to change the views of society all on your own then, Hudson? Or maybe you're going to change the laws so it's legal to have more than one significant other? What kind of crap do you want me to believe? David Lassiter can't even marry the man he loves in this state. A man he's been with for nearly thirty years, and you're telling me that somehow the world is just going to accept you, me, *and* your three brothers?"

As she spoke her voice grew louder and her temper flared. All of her fears and her own anxiety at how this weekend would change her life was coming out of her in one angry blow. Hudson released her chin, and stepped backwards silently. Reaching for a towel he handed it to her and then grabbed another to wrap around his waist before meeting her gaze again.

"Rachel, you're right. Society as a whole doesn't get it, but what do you care what people think? You're a fiercely independent woman who is forging her own way, with a bright career and a solid place in this community. So why would you let anyone dictate who you love?"

She couldn't answer him. His words stuck in her heart like an assassin's blade. When her mother told her that her father was leaving them for another woman, and another family, a piece of her heart had died a slow death. There were rumors that kept the gossip hounds circling for months as the divorce was processed through the courts, and alimony and child support checks were argued. The kids at school whispered the things they heard their parents say, and the ladies in town watched her and her mother with pity in their eyes. She had sworn in those days that she would never let other people tell her how to live her life, yet here she was using society's opinions to dictate her decisions. It was a painful truth, but there it was.

Refusing to let him see how much he had shaken the stability of her arguments, she turned and walked out of the bathroom to the bedroom to redress. No matter what, she was leaving this house tomorrow. She was going back to her life, and she was going to allow herself the time to figure out exactly what she needed. Four possible heartbreaks stood between her and the door, but there was nothing she could do about it. Her mind was made up.

****

A couple of hours later Rachel sat snuggly tucked in between Rogan and Parker on the sofa, while Sawyer sat in front of her with her legs over his shoulders. Hudson was sprawled out in a chair with his long legs propped up on the coffee table, and a bottle of beer in his hand. They were watching *X-Men* and even though Rachel wasn't a huge fan of the movie, she was a big fan of the moment. Parker's fingers were playing with her hair as she rested in the crook of his arm, and Rogan's thumb was tracing circles in the palm of her hand where he held it in his lap. A big bowl sat on the floor nearby, empty but for a few un-popped kernels of popcorn.

All of this sex was bound to take a toll on her body, and she was definitely tender, but it was the most pleasurable pain she could imagine. Every time she shifted, the material of the t-shirt she snatched from Parker's dresser rubbed against her bruised lower back, and when she shifted her legs she felt the pull of muscles in her thighs and ass. Excruciatingly sensual, and delightfully decadent. No matter that it was almost over, or that she would never get to experience it again. She just wanted to enjoy every second of it while it lasted.

The credits began to roll and she shifted positions, pressing her head against the solid wall of Parker's chest and inhaling his scent deep into her lungs. He pressed a kiss to the crown of her head surprising her, and she tipped her head to look up into his dark eyes.

"You doing okay, sunshine? Tired?"

His concern for her made her throat tighten, but she forced out a small smile. "I'm good, a little tired, but I could probably handle another movie. I'm not ready to move yet."

Parker's grin of pleasure surprised her even more. He was normally such a hard ass, so it was wonderful seeing him act normal. "You got it, Rach. Do you want to pick this time?"

Rachel laughed when all three of his brothers groaned. "Hey! How do you guys know I'll pick a movie you don't want to watch?"

"It's inevitable. You're female," Sawyer said despondently, and Rachel smacked the back of his head.

"You weren't complaining about that this morning now, were you, lover?"

Sawyer flipped on her, knelt between her knees, pressing her back into Parker as he took her mouth in a hot kiss. When they broke apart he winked, "Never, baby. I wouldn't dare complain about your female parts. Now, pick a movie while I make more popcorn. Hudson can get you another drink."

Rachel accepted the hand he held out so she could rise from the couch and she headed for the bookshelf full of DVDs. Scanning the titles she could feel Parker and Rogan watching her from behind. Feeling just a twinge of naughty, she rose up on her toes to reach for the highest shelf. The t-shirt she wore rose up, exposing the crease of her ass cheeks, and both men groaned. Giggling as she dropped back flat on the floor, she turned to show them her selection.

"Good choice," Parker said with a raised eyebrow.

She handed the movie to him with a wink, "I know what my guys like."

The moment the words left her mouth her stomach dropped to her feet. She had just laid claim. Something she swore not to do, and there was a triumphant look in Parker's eyes that made her knees wobble. Refusing to confront it, she spun on her heel.

"I need to...um...I'll be right back."

Once she was standing in the bathroom with the door locked, she gulped down large breaths of air, and clenched her eyes shut.

You did not just tell them that they were yours!

Her conscience was wavering, because she wanted so badly for her statement to be true. If only it wasn't all four of them. Why couldn't she be normal and fall for just one man who alternately loved her and made her crazy?

After using the bathroom, and splashing water on her face, she forced herself to go back into the living room. The four men were talking in hushed tones until she stepped into the room, and then all eyes were on her. It was very disconcerting.

"Did you really pick out *Lara Croft Tomb Raider*, or is Parker trying to pull a fast one?" Sawyer asked with a grin.

She shook her head and returned the reassuring smile, "Yes, I really picked it out. I like that movie. It has a strong woman who kicks ass in it."

"Hmmm…you just keep surprising us, Rach," Hudson said, grabbing her hand to pull her back to her spot in the middle of the couch.

This time Parker and Rogan switched spots, so Rogan's chest was the one her head rested against, while Parker settled in next to her, hip to hip and thigh to thigh. She couldn't bring herself to look him in the eye, because she was afraid he would see her feelings in her gaze. Instead she focused on Sawyer who playfully tickled the arch of her bare foot before kissing her ankle, and settling her legs comfortably over his shoulders again. His brown hair brushed the insides of her knees, and his hands felt hot on her shins where he gripped her.

The bowl of popcorn was passed to her and she took a small handful, mindful of the fact she had already indulged way too much this weekend in junk food. The movie began to roll, but she couldn't focus on it. Instead the men surrounding her consumed her thoughts, driving her mad with desire and confusion.

"Rach, why are you so tense?" Rogan whispered into her ear, but she knew Sawyer and Parker were at least close enough to hear.

"I'm not. I'm just getting tired I guess."

"We can shut it off if you want to go to bed," Hudson said, looking deeply concerned. Ever since she walked out of the bathroom he had remained slightly distant from her, watching and waiting for her next move. It was disconcerting to say the least. The other brothers hadn't mentioned the argument, although she knew logically they had to have heard it.

She shook her head, "Nah, I'm alright, but if I fall asleep first, you have to promise not to draw a mustache on me, or dip my hand in warm water."

That got everyone laughing, and she relaxed a little. Parker's eyes caught hers and held her gaze. He lifted one eyebrow, "You know, sunshine, it seems like you only get uncomfortable when all four of us are here."

Rogan stiffened underneath her head and she darted a wary glance up at him. Seeing his questioning look, she shrugged. "I don't know. Maybe. I mean, it's not every day a girl has a movie night with four men she has slept with."

"It freaks you out to be with all of us?" Sawyer asked, and she felt guilty for it. There was hurt in his beautiful chocolate eyes, and she reached for him.

"It's not normal, Sawyer. Brothers don't usually have a relationship with the same woman. So yes, it freaks me out." She felt better for saying it, and worse for hurting him as the sparkle in his eyes dimmed further.

"Why did you agree to this weekend, Rach?" Rogan asked, sitting still as stone underneath her.

She let out a heavy sigh, "Honestly? Because you guys have invaded my fantasies on a daily basis for years, and I needed to forget about how much Mitch hurt me."

"So, we're your rebound," Sawyer said, standing abruptly, and then sitting on the coffee table to face her. The movie played on in the background, but all four Brooks brothers were focused on her now.

"No! It's not like that for me! I mean, well…in a way I guess you are a rebound, but it's not like I just randomly picked someone. I was going to you know? I was going to have a one-night stand last night with whomever I could pick up, but then you guys showed up, and asked me to walk on the wild side. I couldn't say no. I wanted you." She held her head up, meeting each man's gaze steadily and refusing to cower in shame for what she felt.

"So it meant nothing to you. It's all just been about trying something new?" Parker snapped, and it tore into her as painfully as if he had shoved a knife in her heart.

"Parker, I have wanted you guys for years. You four walk around this town like you own it, because you know every red-blooded woman within a hundred miles of it wants you. I'm just a woman. I can't promise you more than this weekend. I told you that."

"Why are you so afraid of what you want, Rach?" Rogan said. His voice was the voice of reason. His question perfectly logical and calm, there was no anger, or hurt, or disappointment. Just pure curiosity.

"Wouldn't you be hesitant after someone betrayed you? What if it didn't work out, how would I ever face you four again? I live here, I work here, and I'm not planning to leave, so I need to keep my reputation clean. This is too far out of the box." She wrapped her arms around her middle, feeling particularly vulnerable now that she had said her piece.

"Why do you care what the town thinks? There are other people living in poly relationships around here. They just don't advertise it," Rogan said, still maintaining that unruffled calm demeanor. It was really starting to tick her off, especially hearing the same words from his mouth that Hudson had used earlier to shake her.

"What the hell is a poly relationship?" she snapped. Tears of guilt were burning behind her eyelids, and her mouth was dry again.

"Polyamorous. It means to have more than one partner. I know it isn't exactly common, but we've talked for years about sharing one woman amongst the four of us. We are all voyeurs, so watching our woman getting fucked is a hell of a turn on. Once we started sharing women between us, there was no going back, we just had to find the right woman. One who could appreciate having four very different men in her life." Rogan spoke, but Rachel's eyes were once again captured by Parker.

"Can we please go back to the movie. This is too much for me right now," she whispered, trying to keep the tears of discomfort away. They couldn't know how much she ached to be able to accept a place in their lives. It would hurt him even more when she left tomorrow.

Parker watched her for another minute, and then stood and held out his hand. She frowned up at him in confusion. "If we only have tonight and tomorrow then, I want to do something more intimate than watch a movie. Come."

His demand wasn't unrealistic, and it actually sent a shiver of pleasure down her spine. She had spent time with each of the brothers that she considered "safe," and now it was time for Parker to get some alone time. Parker was darker, more dramatic and dangerous in personality. Something about him told her he would make the night memorable, and that was the reason she stood, following him into his bedroom. He was right, if she only had tonight, she wanted to use it to her full advantage.

Chapter Eleven

Parker's heart was racing in his chest as he led Rachel back to his bedroom. He knew his brothers would stay put and allow him this time with her alone, but the fear that it might be his last time with her made him desperate. If he came on too strong he would scare her, and it was the last thing he wanted to do.

Drawing her into the room behind him, he sat her on the edge of his four-poster bed, and put his hands on her shoulders to hold her still. The height of the bed was perfect for him to fit right between her thighs, but first they had to talk.

"Rachel, you know I'm not like my brothers. I can get a little bit…"

"Bossy? Demanding? Controlling?" He grinned at her response, and she laughed. "Yes, Parker, I know you are different. Each one of you are different, but it's kind of nice. Like getting four different toppings on my ice cream sundae."

The mental image made him groan and he shoved his hand through his hair as he searched for the right words. "Rachel, I'm a Dominant."

Her eyes narrowed and she cocked her head. "Exactly what does that mean?"

"It means that I need to be in control in the bedroom, and I want you to submit to me. I want to know you trust me with your body and your pleasure. I want to make you come a dozen times, but only at my command. It fulfills something inside of me when a woman submits."

"I'm not sure I understand. You want me to lay here and do nothing while you work me over?"

He shook his head, "No, never. I always want you to respond and enjoy yourself. It's so hard to explain. You know what BDSM is right?" When she nodded, he relaxed a little. "Well I practice dominance and submission. I want to tie you up so you can't touch me back. I want to feel your ass under my hand as I spank you. I want to tease you to the point of orgasm and then stop, only to do it again until we both go crazy with need. I want you to acknowledge that your body is mine when you're with me, so I can control your pleasure."

Parker waited for half a breath so she could absorb what he was saying, and then continued, "It's not just about spanking you though. I've watched you build your career, and you are a powerhouse. Woman, you take control over situations and make things happen that no one else could dream of. I want you to let me have that precious control. I want you to let me take care of you and ensure you're pleasure and satisfaction because it will benefit us both."

"Wow…um…okay. Give me a minute to think. I've never…I mean…"

She stayed silent for a few more moments as she processed what he said, and he felt the tension building between them. If she turned him down it would kill him.

"The last time I let someone make decisions for me, he walked away from me and my mother and never looked back."

Parker nodded his acknowledgement of her pain, but didn't question her further. This had to be her decision. He wouldn't ever be happy knowing he forced it upon her. When she abruptly stood in front of him and lifted on her toes to press a kiss to his jaw, he flinched.

"If it's what you need, Parker, then I will try. Believe me, you are the only man I would trust enough to do this with, and you will probably have to walk me through it, but I'm willing to try."

In an instant all of his fears of rejection dissipated. She was agreeing to submit, and it made his cock turn to concrete in his jeans. He had to dig his fingernails into his palm to keep from reaching for her. It was too important they communicate before they played. "Okay, let's set a couple of ground rules and we'll work from there. If at any time you want me to stop, say the word Red, and everything will stop. If you need me to give you a minute to catch your breath or you're uncomfortable, say the word Yellow. The word Green would be everything is okay, so if I ask you what color you are I want you to be completely honest, okay?"

She nodded, and he frowned. "You also have to verbalize. When we're playing I want you to call me, Sir."

Rachel let out a little giggle and then clapped her hand over her mouth. "I'm sorry, I messing this up already. I'll try to do better…Sir."

Shaking his head and rolling his eyes at her reply, he reached for her hands. "Last thing, whatever you do you have to trust me not to hurt you. I…care deeply for you and I would never hurt you."

He saw her eyes widen slightly at his near slip of the tongue, but she just whispered, "Yes, Sir."

Pulling her with him, he stood her at the foot of the bed that dominated the room, right in front of the large cedar chest that held his grandmother's handmade afghans. Tugging his t-shirt from her body he had to bite back a grin at her shiver of anticipation when the cool air hit her naked skin. In the dim lamp light of the room she looked like a goddess standing there naked by his bed. Gently he indicated she should turn around to face the cedar chest, and he bit back a groan at the view. Her hair trickled down her slim back in waves, until it was dancing just above that sexy daisy tattoo and giving him all kinds of delicious ideas for how to use its length to his advantage. The curve of her hips taunted his tongue, and the rosy pink color of the blush on her skin made his cock diamond hard.

"Stay here," he commanded and then went to his closet to get his toy bag. He was going to give Rachel Morgan a night to remember.

****

Rachel didn't know what to think. Dominance and submission was something kinky people did, and she had never experienced it. She was trying not to tremble with the fear and anticipation rolling through her body. Her every nerve was on high alert as she watched Parker disappear into the closet.

He had said he wanted to tie her up and spank her, and surprisingly it didn't scare her. It turned her on. Well, kind of. If she was honest with herself, it left her feeling hot and cold. Who really enjoyed being spanked? The scarier part was he wanted her complete trust in him.

The thought was bouncing through her brain as Parker returned carrying a black duffle bag. He set it down near the edge of the bed and withdrew two lengths of white rope from it. Fear rippled through her as he stepped closer to her naked body, and she turned to face him, reaching out for reassurance with her hand. He pressed a kiss to her palm before releasing her grip, and then met her eyes.

"Do you trust me, Rachel?" he asked in a steady voice that belied the racing pulse she could see in his throat. He was just as nervous and excited as she was. How could she deny him?

"Yes...Sir. I trust you."

He smiled, and turned her back around so her back was to him and she was facing the foot of the bed again. The cold wood of the blanket chest separated her from the carved footboard of the bed and pressed against her knees, but it was tolerable. Quickly and efficiently he wrapped the rope around her wrist and knotted it. To her surprise the rope was soft and silky against her skin, and he left it loose enough that it didn't hurt her. Once the rope was tied to her wrist, he took the other end and tied it to a bedpost. Following suit, he tied the other rope to her opposite hand and the opposite bedpost. She was tied as though on a cross, one wrist to each bed post, her body arching slightly over the blanket chest in an awkward way.

Parker seemed to immediately notice her discomfort, as he moved away to grab a bed pillow and drop it on the bench in from of her. "Here you are, kneel here, Rachel."

A rush of pleasure went through her at his concern for her comfort, and at that moment she realized she really did trust him. There was no doubt in her mind she would enjoy whatever game he wanted to play. Parker was a man of his word, and if he said he wouldn't hurt her, then she should just sit back and relax under his hand.

After she was settled, he finished tying the ropes, tugging on them a little to make sure they were secure. His hand drifted down her arm, and then down the length of her spine, brushing her hair aside and sending tingles of desire rushing to her clit.

"What color are you, sunshine?"

"Green. Uh…Sir."

"Good, just relax." His words whispered over the skin near her ear, and he kissed her shoulder gently. She jumped a little when his hand suddenly came down on her ass with a loud crack. The yelp that escaped her throat was created more by surprise than by actual pain. In fact, a burning sensation seemed to seep through her skin and into her soul as he rubbed his palm over the tender spot for a moment.

He spanked her again, this time on the other cheek, and she bit off the cry of surprise before it released. "Don't hide your response, Rachel. I like hearing your sounds of pleasure, and even the sounds of pain. If you don't respond, then I don't know what pleases you."

She started to nod and then remembered his request that she verbalize. "Yes, Sir. I haven't ever been spanked. Not even as a child." Her voice was raspy and breathless. Like the heat from his hand scorched her vocal chords.

"Mmm…spanking can be used for discipline, or it can be used for pleasure. I prefer the latter of the two options." He brought his hand down on the split of her ass this time, and she groaned as her pussy gushed moisture between her thighs. She could feel it running down the inside of her thigh.

Parker stepped away from her to his bag, and she tried to look over her shoulder to see what he was doing. She caught a glimpse of something pink and a bottle that looked like lube before he was back behind her and out of her view again.

"Trying to sneak a peek? That would ruin the surprise, Rachel."

Cold gel oozed into the crack of her ass, slipping between her cheeks to coat her asshole. The lube was scented and she grinned at the fragrance of cinnamon, wondering if it was flavored too. She would love to test that out on Parker's cock sometime.

Just as she was imagining a mouth full of dick, she felt his finger pressing into her anus, stretching her. She gasped and whimpered a little at the sting as he pushed another finger in and spread them out. Her body relaxed slowly to the intrusion, and as soon as she was taking his fingers easily, he took them away. Rachel's protests were cut off by something blunt and hard pressing against her tiny rosebud. A butt plug. The cold plastic was coated with more lube based on how easily he was able to maneuver it into place, and she swallowed hard at the full burn that enveloped her as he filled her ass.

"Parker!" She was panting now, and finding it hard to keep her eyes open as pleasure and pain rushed through her.

"Easy, love, what color are you now?" His voice was firm and steady, and she latched on to it. Focusing on it and trying to determine if she needed him to stop or if she was just startled by the new experience.

"Greenish Yellow," she mumbled, and he laughed.

"Thank you for being honest, sunshine. I wanted to make it easier on you for later. That's why you have the plug. I want to prepare you for later when I show you the real benefits of having four men available for your pleasure."

Her heart jumped at the thought of having sex with all four of them at the same time. She only had so many places for a cock to go, how exactly would she please four men at once?

"Rachel, come back to me. Get out of your head, and pay attention. You wouldn't want to hurt my feelings while I have you tied up like this." He reached around her to cup her breasts, and she moaned when he pinched her nipples.

"Now that you're settled again, let's move on?"

Parker moved quickly to retrieve something behind her, and then he was behind her again. This time instead of playing with her breasts, he slid his hand down to cup her pussy. His finger slid between her puffy pussy lips easily finding the swollen nub there and circling it ever so gently. It dawned on her that he was being extra gentle with her because he knew she was sore after all the sex this weekend, and she felt her heart expand a little to let him in.

The buzz of vibration hit her ears just before it hit her clit, and this time she jerked in her bonds. "Easy, sunshine." His voice caressed her ear as he slid the vibrating egg into her pussy. As wet as she was, it was no chore sliding easily into her tight cavity. Now she was full. Full and vibrating. She was glad she was kneeling instead of standing, because her knees were wobbling, it was almost too much to take.

"Parker! I can't," she gasped, her eyes clenching and reopening as she tried to work through the vibration of sensual pleasure rolling over her body.

"You can, Rachel. You're so much stronger than you think." After another moment he shut off the vibration and stroked his hand over her flanks gently, soothingly. "See, you're amazing and you don't even realize it."

Her head tipped back on her shoulders as she stared up at the plain white ceiling of his bedroom. In her peripheral vision she could see the rope binding her to the bed on either side of her, and she could feel him nearby, waiting for her to react.

"Why do you need this, Parker? I would make love to you willingly, why do you need me tied down."

There was a pause and she heard his body hesitate before he stepped back up against her, using his palm to turn her head so she would meet his eyes. "I only need your trust, but I gain pleasure from your submission. Every time I bring you to the edge, I'm bringing myself there as well. I'm fighting the urge to shove my cock into your pussy and give us both a quick release, but if I allow myself to give in, we won't reach the heights we will reach if I maintain control. Now, you said you would try. What color are you, Rachel?"

His dark eyes held her captive, and she trembled in her bonds. Her legs were free from restraint, but they were weakening with every new thing he shared. She wanted to see where he would take her. She wanted to know how high she could climb before the fall. With a deep breath, she gave him a small smile. "I'm green, Sir. Do your worst."

Fire flared in the depths of his eyes, and he captured her mouth in a violent kiss that clashed teeth and tongues into a battle of power. He pushed her, but she pushed back, refusing to cower until the vibration flared again deep inside of her cunt. Parker used one hand to gently tap on the base of the anal plug. Again and again he urged her up to the top, only to stop everything and allow her to fall back to the ground. The cycle would start again, sometimes with him spanking her, or pinching her clit, or plunging the anal plug in and out of her ass. It was amazing how much her body was able to take, before she broke. The climax was unexpected and overwhelming. She couldn't even scream because her body was so swallowed up into the sensations.

When she finally sagged against him, her shoulders ached from the pull of the ropes, and her knees weren't strong enough to hold her any longer. Heart racing, and panting for air, she whimpered when he released the ropes and scooped her into his arms.

Moving her to the bed, he laid her down gently, and adjusted her so he fit between her thighs against her spasming pussy. She could feel the sticky wetness of pre-cum on her thigh where his cock pressed against her, and she wiggled trying to signal her desire to have him inside of her.

"No. I say when we continue, Rachel. Lie still while I taste you." His head dipped between her legs before she could respond, and she screamed when his tongue coasted over her clit.

His breath was hot against her swollen labia as he panted his own desire, "What color are you, Rachel?"

It took her a moment to figure out what he was talking about, but she finally managed to gasp out, "Green, Sir, green, green, green…"

Like a mantra, she said it until her brain couldn't form the word anymore. Parker's tongue was like a sexual weapon he used to find her most secret places and expose them. Her body clenched and tightened under his onslaught, but just when she thought she would have another orgasm, he pulled away and surged up onto his knees, thrusting underneath her hips and lifting them so her bottom half was draped over his lap, legs spread. Leaning forward, he held her wrists in one hand over her head, and pushed his cock into her pussy.

The angle of their bodies meant he was pressing against her G-spot with every thrust, and she felt hot tears rolling down her cheeks. The fire inside of her was too big and too hot for her to control it, so she let it go. She gave it to him, submitting to his pounding body, and letting him steal her soul.

When he finally gave in to his own climax she screamed out his name, hearing it ringing in her ears long after her voice was spent. She was barely awake when Parker settled her under the covers on his bed, and left her for a moment to clean up. A warm cloth wiped away the stickiness of her own passion, before he spooned his large body behind her, wrapping her in a cocoon of warm man. She sighed with pleasure as his comfort soaked into her skin, right before sleep swallowed her.

Chapter Twelve

When the morning sun woke her up, Rachel found herself pinned between Sawyer and Hudson in Parker's bed. She could feel Sawyer's heart beating under her cheek, and Hudson's warm breath tickling the tiny hairs on her neck. Amazingly she was very comfy spooning with the two of them.

A small stretch proved she had some unusually sore muscles, but the memories of how each muscle was used made the pain bearable. Her tentative movements seemed to rouse certain baser instincts in her men, as she felt Hudson's cock twitch against her backside, and Sawyer's slow breathing caught and held for a moment. His gorgeous brown eyes fluttered open and met hers almost instantly.

"Morning, baby," he murmured in a rough sexy sleepy voice.

"Good morning. I'm sorry, I don't even remember you two getting into the bed last night." She shivered as Hudson pressed a kiss to the nape of her neck, and his morning whiskers scratched her sensitive skin.

"You were sleeping pretty good. We figured Parker wore your ass out."

"In more ways than one," she responded, snickering and stretching again, arching her back so her ass rubbed against Hudson's groin.

Hudson's groan made her pussy cream and her blood heat. "Oh, honey, you are asking for trouble this morning."

"Really? What kind of trouble do you have in mind, cowboy?"

Sawyer beat Hudson to it, by turning to face her, and bent as though to kiss her. Without a thought, she threw her hand up to block her mouth, and laughed. "No way, Jose! Not with morning breath. Excuse me, fellas, while I go brush my teeth."

Sawyer stared down at her like she had just told him she was leaving their bed to enter a convent. "Are you kidding?"

When she shook her head in the negative, Hudson started to laugh. "After spending the whole weekend having sex with not one, but all four of us, you are still worried about morning breath?"

Feeling embarrassed and now slightly irritated, she shoved at Sawyer's chest until he backed up a few inches, and she was able to crawl over him and climb out of the bed. As she hurried toward the bathroom door, she had to bite her lip to resist responding when she heard Hudson say, "Well at least we get the reward of watching her walk around naked. Hurry back, Rach, I want to finish what we started."

Several minutes later she was feeling fresh breathed and horny. After a dozen orgasms in the last thirty-six hours, she should be curled up in the fetal position nearly comatose, but instead she was invigorated. How many times over the years had she doubted her feminine appeal? This whole ménage weekend might be temporary, but it was still one hell of an ego boost.

Exiting the bathroom, she found Hudson still reclining on the bed where she left him, but Sawyer was curiously absent. Noting her frown, Hudson was quick to fill in the blanks. "He went to get something to eat for you. He'll be right back. In the mean time…"

She grinned back when he wriggled his eyebrows playfully, and then launched herself across the room and on to the bed. His yelp of surprise was drowned out by her giggles as she bounced on the mattress and then climbed over him until she was straddling him with her hands pressed to his wide chest. "What exactly did you have in mind?"

"Whoa! Who are you and what did you do with my quiet and sedate Rachel?" he asked, with a teasing wink.

"I locked her in the bathroom. I figured you should meet the wild and crazy side before the weekend was out."

"Oh? So she's not the same girl who had her finger up my ass yesterday? And not the same girl who accepted our invitation to share our beds for the weekend then?"

Rachel rolled her eyes at his continued teasing, "Do you want to fuck or talk about my multi-faceted personality?"

A grunt was his response, but his eyes flashed with irritation. "Actually, I want to fuck you *and* talk to you. Is that so bad? Why are you so afraid to talk to me, Rach? Afraid I might find out more about you and still like you?"

She stared down at him in shock. Was he serious? She was naked and sitting on top of him with his semi-erect cock cradled against her already damp pussy, and he wanted to have a relationship talk. This was unbelievable. Pushing off him, she walked wordlessly to Parker's dresser and dug through the drawers until she found a t-shirt to pull on. Once she was covered, she spun back to him and gave him her coldest glare.

"Look, I might not be the sharpest tool in the shed, but at least I'm not living in some sort of fairytale land where everyone accepts everyone else and lives happily ever after. I get it, Hudson, you want a relationship, and to be honest I appreciate that you're so transparent, but let me be crystal-clear. I can't be what you four want. I promised you the weekend, and we only have a few hours left. We can either spend it having dirty raunchy sex and making fantastic memories, or you can just give me the word and I'll get my shit and go."

"Is that all this is to you, Rachel?" Parker's voice was as strong and powerful as ever, but there was a vulnerability in his eyes when she turned to face him in the doorway. He was hurt. Behind him, Sawyer and Rogan were watching the scene solemnly. All four men were waiting for her answer. *How much more fucked up could this get?*

"What do you want me to say, Parker? I didn't come out here with hearts and flowers in my eyes." She stiffened her spine, but when his chocolate brown eyes shuttered and he flinched as if she had physically hit him, she regretted her words. "I'm sorry, that didn't come out right. You guys are just so damn overwhelming. I want you all so much. I've wanted you for years…but just because you want something doesn't mean it's the best thing for you. I wouldn't go on a week-long ice cream binge just because I craved it."

She waited several heartbeats as they all continued to stare at her. A range of emotions flitted through the four men's faces. Hurt, anger, frustration, but there was still desire. She could still feel their desire through it all, burning through her skin and branding her soul.

A silent conversation seemed to happen in the blink of an eye between the brothers, and suddenly Parker was holding his hand out to her. "Rachel, come here."

She went without a second thought. It was like a soldier running for cover when bullets were flying. She knew no matter what happened Parker would protect her from whatever was to come. He was her safe place. Holding his hand, and standing just inches in front of him, she stared at the line of dark hair that sprinkled the center of his chest. His fingers came up and tipped her chin so she had to look up at him.

"Rachel, I'm done playing games. You knew from the beginning we were hoping this would turn into more than just a weekend fling. The sex has been amazing, but we want more. Every time one of us tries to get close to you, you throw up a wall and deflect us. Even in sex, you haven't let us love you yet. You've fucked us, but you're too scared to make love to us. This is it. Make your choice. You can either go to the kitchen, have breakfast while I get dressed, and then I will drive you home, or you let us take you back to that bed and make love to you. All four of us. If you choose the first option, know that it will be over. We will not pursue you once you leave this house. But, if you choose the second option, you must open yourself up to us. At least give us a chance to show you how much we..." his breath caught as he broke off for a second, "give us that much, please?"

It could have been moments or it could have been an hour. Rachel was captivated by the seriousness of Parker's words, and the emotions that swirled in the depths of his dark gaze. He was offering her an out, but she wasn't sure she was strong enough to take it. The temptation to let them make love to her was just too big.

She heard herself whisper, "Make love to me."

A spark of fire seemed to pass from Parker to her as he bent forward and brought his lips just millimeters from hers before whispering back, "With pleasure, sunshine."

Rachel only knew Parker's lips for the next few moments as he nearly swallowed her whole, devouring her, and claiming her in the same viciously passionate kiss. There were hands on her body, and the slight feeling of weightlessness before the cold sheet brushed her skin and her head dipped into a pillow.

All at once, hot palms skimmed over her thighs, callused fingertips slid up under her t-shirt to pinch her nipples, and her hair was tugged possessively to tip her head back and bare her throat for seeking lips.

There was no escaping the sensual onslaught as they took control and made love to her body. No skin went untouched, or unkissed, and she felt like she was spinning in a vortex of debauchery. Fingers dipped between her thighs, teasing her clit and spreading her juices to her asshole before disappearing. Her focus was torn between the four brothers and she finally just closed her eyes and let go. She relaxed into their hands, letting them have their way with her, letting them take complete control of her need and her desire. This was what they wanted, and if she was honest with herself, she wanted it too.

In her head she heard the racing of her own heartbeat drumming rhythmically through her veins. She heard herself whimpering, and moaning, and even begging for their touch, but she wasn't conscious of any of it. A cloud of passion seemed to take over her, and she let her doubts and questions disappear into the haze.

When one of the brothers spread her knees with his hands, and two others reached to hold her open, she gasped, only to find the fourth brother waiting to capture her breath with his own lips. Rogan. That's whose lips possessed hers. She could taste him, and smell the scent that was Rogan alone. A brush of whiskers against her perineum told her it was Hudson's tongue dancing merrily across her labia and clit. He caught her swollen bud between his lips and gently sucked on it, making her cunt spasm and her stomach tighten.

His fingers slid into her channel curling upward to find that deliciously secret spot that sent her exploding into orgasm, but before she could find her climax he eased back, and another set of fingers was brushing her exposed asshole. One of the brothers was teasing her ass, while Hudson continued to eat her pussy, and Parker made love to her mouth. When a hard cock was pressed into her clenching fist, she lost track again so caught up in the whirlwind of heated desire she couldn't focus on who was where or how many hands touched her and teased her.

Fingers were slipping in and out of her body with no resistance, and her breasts were swollen and aching. She needed to be filled completely so she could come.

"Please!" she heard herself begging, but the brothers only seemed more driven to keep her on the edge. They tormented her body, gifting her with all of the delicious attention any woman could ever want, and none of the release.

A rustle of the bed sheets was the only hint of the movements around her as they traded places and duties, taking turns tasting her everywhere. She kept trying to open her eyes and focus on them long enough to note who was where, but her mind seemed determined to avoid it, and even when open her vision was cloudy. Four tongues, four mouths, eight hands, four cocks, all touching her at once, and then disappearing only to reappear in a new territory. Mindlessly she babbled and pleaded in whispers and wails, until one of them broke.

Out of nowhere she felt her body being lifted and she was draped over the top of Sawyer. She would know the grip on her hips anywhere. Her cowboy grinned up at her when she cracked her swollen eyes open and managed to focus her vision on him.

"Come on, cowgirl, giddyup." He lifted her hips, lining his cock up with her pussy, and she heard herself cry out his name as he pulled her down onto him. Never before had she climaxed upon contact, but she couldn't have stopped it this time if she had wanted to. Her body shuddered and bucked on top of him like she was really riding a bull, and he patiently waited her out.

It briefly crossed her mind that his brothers must have quite the view, before she felt one of them spreading some sort of lube over her back hole with his fingers. She must have jumped at the renewed contact because Rogan's voice murmured to her.

"Shhh....it's alright, love. Just relax and let me in." The thick curved head of his cock pushed against her asshole, and she had to force her body to relax and press back against him. When he finally breached the tight ring of muscles, she felt a sigh of relief ripple through him to her and continue through Sawyer. Connected intimately, the threesome began a very slow gentle rocking motion. Neither man seemed in a hurry to reach their release, and since she had already orgasmed once, she had a little ways to go to build back up to another.

Once they were in a steady rhythm, a warm hand on her jaw brought her face up to look at Hudson and Parker who waited next to her with their hard cocks jutting out from their gorgeous bodies. *It should be a sin to look that good naked*, she thought as her mouth watered for a taste of the pre-cum glittering on Hudon's cockhead.

She kept one hand braced on Sawyer's chest, and reached out with the other to grasp Hudson's cock and bring it to her lips. Licking away the drop of moisture made him groan, and she felt warm pleasure fill her chest. Sucking him in deep she steadied herself so he could thrust in and out of her mouth without disrupting the fucking that was going on. A few moments passed and she felt his cock thicken just before he pulled away from her with a curse.

Parker quickly replaced Hudson in her mouth, and began his own version of a fucking rhythm. He was more powerful, more demanding, more raw... Just more. Somehow the change in patterns was the spark to set off fireworks in her belly again, and she began to wriggle on the two cocks that impaled her. Sensing her coming climax,

Sawyer and Rogan sped up their movements while Parker pulled away from her.

"No!" she reached out for him, and he dropped to his knees next to her, gripping her jaw in his hand so their noses were nearly touching.

"Yes, Rachel. Come for me, love."

Just like that, his words ricocheted through her body and her climax exploded. Fireworks flamed behind her eyelids, and molten heat filled her veins. Rogan let out a loud grunt and slammed his cock into her body. She could feel him jerking inside of her as he filled the condom with semen. The flames had barely began to subside when her pulsing body clenched around Sawyer's cock as he too came. His body arched violently up off the bed, lifting the weight of her body and Rogan some as he had his own brilliant orgasm.

They all slumped there for a few moments trying to catch their breath. The emotion of the moment was absolutely turning her world upside down. Trying to determine what happened next, she felt her brain begin to spin.

"No. Rachel, don't do that. You promised to let us in, sunshine, and I'm not in yet." Parker reached over and tugged her from between his two brothers, pulling her up onto her knees in front of him, and wrapping one arm around her slim waist, while his other hand delved into the tangle of her hair.

She had no sense of Sawyer and Rogan moving from the bed, but suddenly Hudson was behind her, pressing against her, and rubbing his hard cock between her ass cheeks. She whimpered and he froze. Realizing he mistook her whimper as a rejection, she wiggled her ass a little until his erection was grinding against her sensitive asshole.

Parker lifted her, forcing her legs to wrap around his lean hips so he would have easier access to her dripping cunt, and then he moved both hands to cup her ass cheeks, spreading her wide for his brother. Her eyes widened as Hudson eased inside of her, and with every precious inch he pushed in, she saw the flames of lust grown in Parker's eyes. By the time Hudson was balls deep inside of Rachel's ass, she wasn't sure she would be able to handle Parker's need it was so great, but he once again surprised her by tenderly kissing her lips and slowly pushing into her pussy. It took Parker longer to sink into her than it had Hudson, and by the time he was all the way inside of her, her head was thrown back on Hudson's shoulder and she was babbling out the mantra, "yes, oh God, please, oh yes."

Once again she was carried up the mountain of passion on the wings of desire as they drove her to heights she couldn't have imagined possible for her exhausted body. In the end she must have blacked out, because she could have sworn she heard whispers of "I love you" in her ears as she drifted off into nothingness.

****

Rachel woke up alone in Parker's bed. Her body physically hurt, but that wasn't the worst of her pain. What hurt the most was the wound she knew was going to scar her heart when she left the Brooks brothers behind.

She was in love with them. No doubt about it. Parker's plan had backfired. Instead of making this easier for them all, it was actually going to make it that much harder.

Her bag lay on the cedar chest at the foot of the bed, and she sat staring at it for several long moments remembering the ease at which Parker was able to obtain her submission and how much she actually enjoyed giving it to him. In the back of her mind a scared little voice reminded her that with trust came heartbreak, and the fantasy time had ended.

Rising from the bed, she dressed quickly, and made her way down the hallway. She could hear the men laughing and chatting in the kitchen as they waited for her to rise and join them. Their light-hearted banter nearly maimed her as she paused just inside the living room, debating what her next move would be.

She couldn't walk in there and pretend as if everything had changed. There was still the small matter of how illegal this kind of relationship was, and how unacceptable it was to pretty much all of society. She may say out loud she didn't care what people thought, but she still had a career to think about.

Instead of facing them in the kitchen, she found herself walking out the front door in search of fresh air so her thoughts didn't suffocate her. She stopped at the edge of the porch stairs unwilling to step out into the sunshine and leave them completely behind. There was a pull deep in her chest to go back in there, and sink into the arms of one of the other brothers.

To let them soothe away the unease that Parker's experiment had caused inside of her. But to do it would be admitting that Parker and Hudson were right. It would be admitting she felt something for them, and she wasn't ready to be that vulnerable again after the events of the last several hours.

"Are you okay, Rachel?" Rogan's voice skittered over her jumpy nerves, and she held her ground, refusing to turn around and face him. Instead she just nodded, silently staring out into the vast nothingness of the grassy fields.

Rogan moved up behind her, but he didn't touch her. He was close enough she could feel the heat from his body through her clothing. Her traitorous libido reacted to his nearness, and she felt her pussy grow wet. This was ridiculous. No man should have this kind of power over a woman, and yet she was surrounded by them.

She moved down the porch steps, and took a seat on the bottom step, putting much needed distance between them.

"Rachel, what happened earlier..."

"What? What exactly happened earlier, Rogan?" she snapped, tossing her hair over her shoulder, and flashing an irritated glare at him.

The frown on his face grew deeper, but he moved closer, taking a seat on the steps next to her. "I thought we made it pretty clear how we felt, but..." his voice fell off when she didn't respond.

If she stayed another minute, there was no way she would be able to avoid getting her heart broken times four. Four men equaled four painfully tragic break ups. Besides, this whole weekend was meant to be a fun exploration of herself, not the beginning of a happily ever after.

"Rachel, talk to me," Rogan's voice brought her back to the front porch steps, and she tipped her head up to the sun, soaking in its heat. It was a sign that nothing had changed. She could still hear the imagined whispers of love in her ears as she stiffened her resolve. If they weren't strong enough to say it when she was face to face with them, well then, she wasn't going to let it concern her either.

She stood, and turned to face Rogan. "Rogan, this weekend has been...memorable, thank you."

Really she meant to walk away and leave it at that, but Rogan was having none of it. Faster than lightning he was on his feet and grabbing her arm to spin her back around so she had to face him. "Are you fucking kidding? Memorable? Thank you? That's all you have to say after the last two days?"

The blood drained from her face as she stared into his dark eyes. Hurt radiated out of him, and she felt terrible for it. "I don't know what you want me to say, Rogan. It's been amazing, sexy, erotic, delicious, mind blowing...a million adjectives would describe it and yet not one word can do it justice, but I need to leave now. I promised you all the weekend, and now it's time for us all to get back to the real world. Let me go, Rogan, you don't want this."

"I don't want this? Do you even hear yourself? You have four of us who want to be everything you could possibly need, and you're going to just walk away?"

Honest anguish was hard to overlook, but Rachel knew she was doing the right thing. She couldn't stay. Once these four realized how the community would look down on them for this kind of relationship, they would break it off, and rip her heart out.

So what if other people did it all the time. Those people didn't have lives and careers built on the kindness of the people in this community. A town where she had lived her whole life.

"Yes, Rogan. I'm going to just walk away like we agreed to when I said I would come out here Friday night. One weekend, with no talk of tomorrow. No promises that can be broken, no feelings that can be hurt, and if you don't let me walk away we'll both regret it."

She turned and walked into the house, hesitating when she again heard the other three brothers' voices in the kitchen. Instead of facing them she walked deliberately down the hallway to get her things from Parker's room. Flashes of her pleading and begging the four men to make love to her threatened to overwhelm the tentative grip she had on her decision, so she rushed to collect her things and phone the one person she knew wouldn't judge her actions. Her best friend, Zoey.

It felt like hours but mere minutes passed before Zoey's battered sedan came rumbling down the Brooks brothers' drive. Rachel stood on the edge of the porch trying to decide whether or not she should go back inside the house and say goodbye, or just leave. Ultimately, she needed a clean break to protect her own shaky heart, so she walked away.

Down the steps. One…two…three…four…to the pavered walk that lead to the drive. Her bag clutched in her grip like a lifeline, and her eyes boring into the questioning gaze of her closest confidant.

"What's going on, Ray?" Zoey's concerned voice nearly broke down the line of Rachel's spine, but she managed a sharp shake of her head as she climbed into the car.

Before Rachel could second-guess her decision, Zoey had them turned around and flying back down the gravel drive. In the side mirror, Sawyer and Rogan stood on the edge of the front porch—one looking furious, and one looking heartbroken.

It was on the edge of her tongue to tell Zoey to turn back, but the memory of Mitch's perfidy still burned in her brain. She couldn't take it if any of the four Brooks brothers let her down, and it was inevitable if she stayed. Without another look back, she turned to Zoey and began to share all of the sordid details of the weekend.

Chapter Thirteen

Hudson couldn't believe that Rachel had actually left. The whole weekend had gone nuclear and he didn't have a clue how to fix it. All he wanted was to make her feel wanted and desired, yet somehow they had hemmed her in and made her feel claustrophobic and paranoid. So she ran as fast as her sexy slim legs and black cowboy boots could carry her, right out of their lives. It was a disaster.

Now Parker was pissed, Sawyer was sulking, and Rogan was…well…Rogan was in a daze on the front porch staring down the road in the direction that Zoey's car had taken Rachel. Hudson wasn't sure what his own reaction was. He felt like someone had shoved a fist into his chest and yanked out his heart by brute force. A lonely sense of abandonment filled his stomach, and when he caught a glimpse of himself in the side-mirror on the car, all he saw was a vast nothingness in his own eyes. He was nothing without Rachel. They were nothing without her.

In a strange way, this whole weekend had sealed the deal for him in terms of who he wanted to spend the rest of his life with. He had absolutely no doubts about his choice, but knowing she had doubts was killing him.

After she left, Hudson sat in the kitchen at the dining room table thinking back through the entire weekend, and wondered if there was anything they might have done differently to give her more security.

Ultimately, he gave in and popped the top on a can of beer before he headed into the back bedroom where the five of them had spent the last couple of hours in sexual euphoria. Ropes still hung from the bedposts, and lying at the foot of the bed on the floor, was a shiny silver belt buckle in the shape of a star. It winked at him, teasing him with what might have been, and he had to swallow back the burn of tears behind his eyelids.

As he picked it up and slid it into his pocket, a sense of determination began building in his gut. Rachel was his woman. She might not completely understand it yet, but she wasn't going to find it easy to just walk away from the Brooks brothers without a backwards glance.

Within minutes he was in his truck and headed into town, a plan already formulating in his brain. This love story wasn't over yet.

****

After hours at Zoey's place moping and moaning about her heartache, her best friend had done what only a good best friend could do. She kicked Rachel out and told her she was being stupid.

Of course, Rachel didn't listen, and chose to go home instead of driving herself back to Brooks Pastures. She wasn't willing to risk getting hurt by those four men, even if Zoey thought she had found her soul mates. There was just too much at stake.

However, seeing a bouquet of white lilies waiting for her on the porch, along with a tiny white envelope, left her feeling like a heel for the hurt she was causing the four of them. If there was any way to avoid it, she would, but in this particular situation, she had to choose between protecting her own heart and protecting theirs.

The note was simple, and hand written. It said, "Rachel, We'll be here when you're ready. Love, Hudson."

It was kerosene to the flames of sorrow already burning inside of her. *Hudson*. Sweet, kind, gentle Hudson somehow understood she left because she was scared. It meant more to her than she could have verbalized, and it was a good thing no one else was around because the tears began flowing like a river again.

She spent the rest of the day torn between tears and determination. Space and time. That was what she needed to let go the weekend, and forge ahead into the future. If there was an easier way, she would have gladly jumped on it, but the only thing she felt she could do was pretend like nothing had happened. Zoey was the only one that knew about the weekend's antics, and that was how Rachel wanted it to be.

Except that every couple of days, she received a new little reminder from them. There were lilies the first day, a bottle of bubble bath in her mailbox on Thursday, a bag of SweeTarts showed up on her desk at work the following week, and so on and so on. The only note she ever received was the one from Hudson that Sunday afternoon, but she knew he had a big hand in the other gifts.

Each time she found a new surprise her resolve weakened, but yesterday was the kicker. When she got home from work there was a small gift bag tied to the front door handle. Inside she found a tiny pink box that held the most delicate silver charm bracelet. There were only four charms dangling from the pretty links, a silver heart, a cowboy hat, a pair of handcuffs, and a teddy bear. Her heart had nearly burst out of her chest as she took in the four reminders. One for each man, and each with more significance than they probably even knew.

It was time to admit to herself that loved them more than she could possibly have anticipated. She wanted to be with them, but she had no idea how to take back what she had said, much less what she had done. It was her call to walk away from them, and they were leaving it in her court to come back. If only they understood how hard that was.

****

Two solid months of misery later, Rachel sat in her office with an uneaten handful of saltine crackers next to her computer monitor, and a diet ginger ale in her hand while she waited for her mom to log on to Skype. She spoke with her mom weekly, and every week she had been purposely vague about her love life, so as not to rouse her suspicions. Now, there was no more avoiding it. It was time to make the biggest announcement of her life to her mom.

Rachel was pregnant. There was no denying the four over-the-counter pregnancy tests she had taken, or the doctor's blood test, which assured her she would be having a baby next winter. Her worst nightmare had come true, and she didn't know what to do now.

Her stomach twisted and turned, and she had been nauseous almost since the moment she walked out the door of the Brooks brothers house, so she hadn't realized she had missed her period until just last week. All of her focus had been on avoiding facing any of the four brothers, but now she had to face the reality in front of her, and she had to tell them.

She had pleaded with the doctor to explain how her birth control had failed, only to get a shrug and, "Sometimes, these things just happen." Now, just as she had feared, she had no idea which brother was the father.

There was no way they would want her now. Not when she had rejected them so soundly, and ignored all of their little gifts. She would be lucky if they even acknowledged she was breathing, much less that she carried one of their offspring.

The tinkling sound of her computer drew her back into the real world as her mother came online.

"Hi, sweetheart!"

"Hi, Mama."

"Oh, baby girl, I've missed you."

"I miss you too, Mama."

"You look tired, are you working too hard down there? Maybe you should take a vacation and come up to Oklahoma to visit me."

Rachel snorted out a laugh, "You know I wish I could, Mama, but if I don't work, I don't get paid. I do miss you like crazy though. I actually have some news."

Her mother instantly looked suspicious, and her eyes narrowed. Rachel would have laughed if the situation weren't so serious. "Is this about that Mitch asshole? Is he bothering you again?"

"No, I've told you before that Mitch and I are through. He seems very happy with Connie, and I'm very happy to let her have him. Actually, I haven't spoken to him in a couple of months."

"Okay, so if it's not guy trouble—"

"I didn't say it wasn't guy trouble."

"Aha! So there is a man in your life! I knew you were hiding something. You've been acting strangely ever since you and Mitch split up. Who is it?"

"Do you remember the Brooks family?"

"Brooks Pastures, of course I remember them. I went to school with Susan Brooks. It was terrible when she got sick and died, and then John died shortly after. They had four sons didn't they? Which one are you seeing?"

Rachel set the can of soda down and stared at it, trying to figure out the right words.

"Rachel? What is it honey?"

"Mom, I actually have seen all four of them."

To her surprise her mother laughed, "Good for you! I was worried about you after Mitch was such an asshole. I'm not sure I would have chosen to sneak around with four brothers though."

"No, Mama, you don't understand. I slept with all four of them, at once. It's a long story, but they asked me out to their ranch for a weekend of wild and crazy sex, and I was lost and hurting after yet another shitty end to a shitty relationship, so I said yes, and it was amazing, but now…"

"But now?"

"I'm pregnant."

Her mother's face fell, and she froze in place. After a few seconds, Rachel actually tapped the computer mouse thinking that somehow the computer had frozen.

"Mama, did you hear me? I'm pregnant."

"I heard. I just don't know what to say. I want to congratulate you, because a baby is a blessing but, Rachel, sweetheart, you're so young, and I'm so far away, and wait a second…whose baby is it?"

Rachel just shook her head as tears finally spilled down her cheeks. They were the first tears she had let loose since the day she left the four brothers behind, and they felt horribly good.

"Well this is quite a conundrum. What did they say when you told them?"

"I haven't yet. I don't know how."

"Oh, baby, I wish I could be there to hold your hand and help you through it, but this is something only you can handle. If they were just a weekend fling and they don't want any part of this baby's life, then you will just pack up and move up here with me, and I'll help you raise him or her."

"I can't do that, Mama. My career is here in Texas, and besides, they knew there was a chance when we realized we had forgotten the condom. No, I have to face the music and tell them. I just haven't worked up the courage."

Her mother was silent for several beats.

"Whatever you decide to do, baby, just know that I love you, and I will support you. If you need to come up here and lie low for a bit I have a spare bedroom."

"Thank you, Mama. I love you, too."

"I have to go, sweetheart, but call me as soon as you've told them. Okay?"

Rachel nodded, and waved at her mom before the video screen clicked off. The moment she was alone in the silence of her office she let the leaky dam burst and she cried all of her fear and shame out onto her desk.

Just like her mother, she was alone with a child and walked a precarious line of indecision. Her mother had known about her father's affair for months before he admitted it. Firmly believing he would give up on the tramp he was seeing and come back to his family. When he didn't, it ruined both her and her mother's lives. If the guys decided they didn't want anything to do with Rachel and the baby...well at the moment that was just unimaginable.

Her phone rang, and she reached for it, pleased to see Zoey's name pop up.

"Hey, Zoey."

"Uh oh, did it go that badly? Is your mom pissed?"

Rachel laughed a little, "No, in fact she was very supportive. Concerned for the baby and me, but supportive. She offered to let me move in with her."

"What? You can't go to Oklahoma!"

Now Rachel chuckled a little. "I'm not. She just offered, which was very sweet of her considering she's in a two bedroom place that's barely big enough for her, much less her daughter and a baby."

"So, if she was supportive, why are you crying, Ray?"

Rachel held her breath for a moment, thinking about it. Zoey was as close as a sister to her. They shared all of their secrets, and Rachel had been completely honest with her about why she had been at the Brooks brother's ranch, without going into too much detail about her sexual escapades.

"What if they don't want us, Zoey?"

Zoey's laughter filled her ears, and Rachel frowned at the phone. "Girl, those four have been moping around like wounded animals for two months! They show up everywhere they think you will be, ask everyone about you, leave messages on your phone, send flowers to your door, and otherwise *beg* you to give them a chance. I love you, Ray, but what the fuck is wrong with you?"

Rachel flinched like Zoey had just smacked her in the face. "Excuse me?"

"Rachel Lia Morgan. You are an intelligent woman, and you have found not one, but *four* amazing men who want to love you and care for you, why are you ruining it for yourself?"

"They could break my heart…"

"And the pope could wear a pink tutu for the Easter service, and Brad Pitt could suddenly shave his head and move to Tibet to become a monk, but none of those scenarios are logical or likely, so again I ask, what is your fucking problem? You're talking yourself out of the best thing you've ever had in front of you, because you're afraid of your father."

"He left me, Zoey. If he can walk away from his wife and child to create a whole new family, then why wouldn't these four guys do the same? I barely survived daddy leaving, and every guy I've dated has hurt me by walking away from me—"

"Pfft. Have you ever considered that maybe you pushed them away?"

That stopped Rachel in her tracks and she fell silent.

"Rachel, you have been running from commitment ever since we were kids. Just once, trust your gut and give these guys a chance! I'm not saying you have to marry them, I'm just saying, be honest with them and give them a chance to decide what they want."

Zoey was so right that it irked Rachel, and she refused to respond. Childish, and immature, but damn it she didn't like being wrong. Just because she was pregnant, didn't mean she had to make a long-term decision about her relationship with the guys, and it was still possible they would choose to walk away, right?

Ending her phone call with Zoey, she stiffened her spine and called Rogan.

****

Rogan was dying inside. He and his brothers had walked around like zombies for almost two months hoping Rachel would change her mind, but she hadn't. In fact, she had avoided them all at every turn. Phone calls went straight to voicemail, when they showed up at her office she had her secretary blow them off and hurry them out the door telling them she was at some forgotten 'meeting'.

It was painfully obvious she was just as broken up as they were. She had lost weight, and her eyes had a shadowed, haunted look he had never seen before. When she had spotted him watching her at the diner, she had turned away, and quickly asked for her meal to be boxed up. He hated knowing she was afraid of them in any way. It made him feel like shit.

Hudson hadn't told them about the gifts he was sending her until last week. That was when he had the idea to give her the charm bracelet. He thought if they sent something with more meaning behind it, it just might be enough to crack the icy shell she had built around herself. Rogan never expected it to work when he selected the tiny cowboy hat charm, but right now, he sent up a prayer of thanks for Hudson's brilliance.

Until today, he had nearly given up hope they would be able to get back on the right path with her, but today, Rachel had left a message on their home answering machine. She sounded upset, but her voice still managed to make Rogan's cock hard in his jeans. He hadn't even waited to tell his brothers she had called. He had just picked up the phone and called her back immediately.

She was short with him, but she asked him if she could come to talk to the four of them tonight. It was perfect. They would be able to get her to sit still long enough to hash this whole relationship out, and this time chivalry be damned, he was keeping her until she listened.

Rushing out to the barn to tell Parker the news, he sent Sawyer and Hudson a 911-text message. Parker was knee deep in manure when Rogan found him, but he seemed to sense the urgency and dropped his shovel instantly.

"What is it? What's wrong?"

"It's Rachel, she called and wants to come over tonight to talk. To talk to all of us."

A myriad of emotions crossed Parker's face, and Rogan waited patiently for his reaction. His eyes finally hardened into deep brown pools of pain. "Great, so she's coming to get our hopes up and kick us in the nuts again. Fabulous."

"You don't know that, Parker. Maybe she has been pining away for us too, or maybe she found out she's dying and she needs one of us to donate a freaking kidney. For God's sake, don't fuck this up because you've got your panties in a wad."

Parker's temper flared at the insult. "Fuck you, Rogan. She. Left. Us. Not the other way around. We gave her everything, laid it all out on the table, and she still left. She knew how we felt about her and she still fucking ran."

Rogan silently glared at his brother, absorbing his words and his pain like a sponge. He hadn't realized how hurt Parker had been by Rachel's leaving until this moment. Parker had remained stoic for the most part, acting as though the whole thing had been intended to be temporary. Now, his armor was finally cracking, and Rogan was shocked to find a bleeding heart underneath.

"Parker, did you ever once tell her you loved her?"

Nostrils flaring, Parker nearly growled his answer out, "No. I showed her."

"Well I didn't either, and sometimes words are necessary. Maybe this time instead of fucking her into oblivion, we try being honest and admit we're head over heels in love with her."

"Fine, you tell her whatever the fuck you want, but I'm not sure I'll have much to say."

Rogan snorted at Parker, "Yeah, right. Mr. Dominant always has something to say. Think of it this way, Parker, if she's coming back to ask for our forgiveness, maybe you'll get a chance to spank her ass for leaving in the first place."

Parker's lips lifted in an evil grin, and Rogan laughed out loud as he left the barn and Parker to his wicked thoughts.

Chapter Fourteen

Rachel's heart was racing as she climbed out of her truck, and stood staring up at the Brooks brother's home trying to get her courage together and walk in. They would all four be there, waiting for her as she had requested because that's just how they were. She could feel the cold metal of the bracelet on her wrist, and she played with the tiny charms nervously.

The excitement in Rogan's voice when he answered the phone and agreed to the meeting still left a burning feeling in her heart. Would he be just as enthusiastic when he found out what brought her here?

She wasn't going to lie to herself. There was just as much excitement under her skin at the chance to see the four men as there was anxiety about facing them again. As she started toward the front porch, the screen door creaked open, and she looked up to find Sawyer and Rogan standing in the entryway with mile wide grins on their handsome faces.

Dark eyes followed her path as she took the steps carefully, hoping and praying the trembling in her knees wasn't obvious. Her body flamed to life when Sawyer pushed past Rogan and met her in the middle, wrapping his arms around her and burying his face in her hair with a laugh.

"Good God, woman, I thought you would never come to your senses," he said into her ear and Rachel felt tears burning her eyes.

He held her like a precious childhood toy that gave him comfort and security, clutching her to his chest tightly, but stroking his hands up and down her back at the same time. She couldn't resist turning her face and pressing her nose against his throat to get a whiff of his strong masculine scent. She had missed him. Letting all of the love she had hidden away before flood through her now, she hugged him back without a word.

When he finally lifted his head and noted her watery expression, his coffee colored eyes filled with concerned. "Oh shit, did I hurt you, baby? I was just so glad to see you...I mean to see you here...with us...at our house...fuck!"

She patted his chest with one hand while using the other to brush a stray tear from her cheek. "I'm okay, cowboy. It's just nice to know I was missed."

He gave her his best cheeky grin and stepped back to give her some room to greet his brothers. Rogan was next to wrap her in his arms, hugging her almost as tightly as Sawyer had, and brushing a sweet kiss over her forehead.

"I missed you too, love." he whispered, and she gave him her brightest smile, trying not to let her worry and fear show. Very shortly he would probably be rethinking that statement.

Rogan held the door to allow her through it, and she stepped inside and into Hudson's waiting embrace. His was less comforting than Rogan and Sawyer's had been, and she could see the hurt and confusion that lined his face. Hudson wasn't quite as optimistic about her sudden appearance it would seem.

Rachel's stomach flip-flopped. Rogan at least still had positive feelings toward her, but it was possible this baby was Hudson's and not Rogan's. If that was the case, would the tension always remain between them?

Sensing her hesitation, Hudson gave her a half smile that she assumed was supposed to alleviate her fears, but actually just sent a shaft of pain through her heart. "Welcome back, Rachel."

It killed her that she had been the one to steal Hudson's smile. The sweet romantic man, who had trusted her, now looked down at her like she was a predator on a mission to rip his throat out. It would be a terrible loss for the world if he never regained his happy jovial self.

"Thank you for the gifts," she murmured, and his eyes dropped to her wrist. She had hoped to see a spark of something there, but he just nodded and kept is face eerily blank.

A shiver of nerves skittered down her spine, and she wrapped her arms around her body. When she turned away from Hudson she realized that Parker wasn't there waiting in line to greet her. In fact, he wasn't in the living room at all. Tossing a curious look at Rogan, she was even more stymied when he just reached for her hand to draw her into the kitchen.

Parker was there seated at the table with a cup of coffee in his hands and a blank look on his face. His eyes surveyed her from top to bottom, taking her in, and she knew he noted the physical changes to her body from her weight loss as well as the dark circles under her eyes. A glint of irritation sparked in the brown depths of his gaze, and she struggled to maintain eye contact as she moved into the room.

"Parker," she said, wanting desperately to say more, but not really knowing what to say.

He gave her a nod, "Rachel. You haven't been taking care of yourself."

She let out a sharp laugh and shook her head. "I'm taking care of myself just fine, thank you for your concern."

Turning she met the eyes of each of the other three before she spoke, "Look, something has...well...umm...can we just take a seat so we can talk?"

Rogan nodded, but a wary look crossed his eyes. "Sure, Rach,"

Once everyone was seated, she stared down at her hands clasped together on the table, unsure of how to start. Sawyer came to her rescue, reaching out from next to her, and placing his hand over the top of hers. It brought back memories of the first time he had made love to her on this very table and she felt her pussy clench with desire. Would there ever be a time these guys didn't turn her on just by their proximity?

Taking a deep breath, she looked up and met Rogan's eyes, and then shifted her gaze to Hudson's. They were the two who would ultimately be affected the most by this news.

"I owe you all an apology and an explanation," she said, and she was reassured when Hudson gave her a small smile of encouragement. Clearly she had chosen the right route. "I ran scared two months ago. You four got under my skin, and I didn't know how to handle it. Unfortunately, I handled it very badly."

"We forgive you, baby, just so long as the next time you have a meltdown you promise to come and talk to us instead of running away," Sawyer said, drawing her hand to his lips. She bit her lip at his enthusiastic response.

"I appreciate that, Sawyer, but I'm not finished yet. When you guys ran into me at the bar that night I was looking for a one night stand with a stranger, not a weekend tryst with four friends and neighbors that I had fantasized about since I was in high-school."

"Since high-school, really? Dayum, Rach, you should have said something sooner!" Rogan teased with a wink.

"Please don't joke yet, Rogan. You see, you guys invited me back here and I should have said no based on our friendship alone, but I couldn't. My own wounded pride over Mitch and Connie, and lust, clouded my judgment."

Parker shifted in his seat, and Rachel could tell he was agitated. He was barely keeping his temper in check. She better hurry this up.

"Once I was here, you guys made me feel like I was someone special and I loved every moment. I purposely kept my distance emotionally because I knew it would hurt to leave, and believe me, it did. I should have stuck around and explained things to you guys, but I wasn't even being honest with myself yet. When my father left my mother for another woman, it cut a really big scar into my heart, and I've let that affect my decisions since I was eight years old. I pushed you away because I just knew there was no way I was woman enough for all four of you, and once you four realized it, you were bound to leave me."

"What the hell, Rachel? Not once did any one of us give you any reason to think we would hurt you. We did our best to show you how much we wanted you, and how much we were already in love with you," Parker said in a low hard voice, making Rachel's heart ache and her stomach twist even more.

"I know that now, but at the time I didn't see it."

"So why are you here all of a sudden with a different outlook? You haven't even bothered to accept a phone call or wave hello since you ran out of here that day, what changed?" His dark gaze penetrated her skin and went straight to her soul. She could feel him picking through her brain and it was making her fidgety.

Parker's words had ensnared all three of his brothers, and the foursome was now looking at her silently, expecting an answer.

"I'm pregnant," she whispered.

In that instant, the world shifted. She watched Parker's jaw clench and his eyes go blank, Hudson's face drained of blood while Rogan's lit up with an ear to ear smile, and Sawyer crowed with pleasure. "Are you serious, Rachel? Oh my God, that's amazing!"

"I'm going to be a father? That's the best news, I mean, Sweet Jesus! I don't know how to be a dad—" She had to look away from Rogan and Sawyer's obvious excitement, because she realized Hudson hadn't told his brothers they had had unprotected sex. Rogan had, but Hudson had kept it quiet.

Hudson cleared his throat, and leaned back in his chair. "Ro, I think you better slow down."

"Why? Bro, I'm going to be a dad!" Rogan said, standing and hurrying around the table to pull Rachel up into his arms. He wrapped her tightly against his chest, and cupped her cheek, "I know you're probably scared, but this is fantastic news, Rach. I'm so…I just…thank you, love, for this precious gift."

"Rogan, stop," she said, pushing at his chest. He let go reluctantly, his body tightening with concern at her tone. "Rogan, you weren't the only one I had an accident with."

"The baby could be mine, Rogan," Hudson said quietly from the other side of the table. His elbows were braced on it, and his fingers were buried in his curly black hair so he wasn't even looking at her. Not a good sign.

Rogan looked from her to Hudson and back. His eyes were confused and wary. "Okay, so what's the big deal?"

She felt her mouth fall open in shock. Hell, her chin probably had a bruise from landing on the floor so hard. "Rogan, this baby might be your brother's baby. I won't know who the father is until after it's born."

Rogan's face relaxed into a smile, and his hands came up to cup her cheeks again, holding her head still so she had to look into his eyes. "Rachel, it doesn't matter. I don't care which one of the four of us fathered the baby, as long as you are its mother. Why don't you understand that?"

To say she was stunned was an understatement. Flabbergasted, emotionally bereft, lost in a sea of confusion and shock, but not just stunned. She stared at the oldest of the four Brooks brothers, taking in the laugh lines around his smile, and the short ends of his dark brown hair that curled over his ears waiting for a trim. His large hands held her face firmly, but his touch was gentle, as though he held a butterfly between his fingers.

She couldn't grasp it in her brain. He really truly didn't care whose child she carried, because he knew it belonged to his bloodline. What a remarkable man he was turning out to be. She gave him a smile, and accepted the sweet kiss he brushed over her lips, before turning back to face the fire with Hudson and Parker who still sat stoically at the head of the table. He was as still and silent as a meditating monk, but the tick of a muscle in his jaw gave him away. Emotions were clearly not as calm on the interior as they seemed to be on the exterior.

Hudson looked torn between joy and sheer terror, but since she could relate to both of those emotions she waited a few moments for him to process before she addressed him.

"Hudson, how do you feel?"

He started to shake his head, and then abruptly stopped and stood. Moving slowly around the table, he stopped in front of where she stood with her back pressed to Rogan's chest. "Rachel, I've known for nearly four years that my body wanted you, but until you were here under our roof, and in my bed, I didn't know how much my soul wanted you. Any child that is part of you is welcome and wanted in my life, whether the baby is half mine or half Rogan's by blood."

Rachel nearly wept as Hudson opened his arms to her. The two men she had been most frightened of their reactions, were happy and content to take on the responsibility of a child. That left Parker who seemed to have shut down on them. Forcing herself just to enjoy the bliss of the moment, she began answering the questions Hudson, Rogan, and Sawyer started peppering her with.

"When is the due date?"

"Next winter."

"Have you called the doctor? Is the baby healthy?"

"Yes and yes, as far as they can tell from blood work."

"When will you know if it's a boy or a girl?"

"Not for a while I guess. I don't know, I'm new to this too. Look, I have my first real OB appointment in a couple of weeks, and you're both welcome to go with me, but there are a few more things to work out."

"Like what?" Rogan asked.

"Well now that I know you want to keep it—"

Sawyer scoffed, and Hudson and Rogan looked horrified, "Did you really think we wouldn't?"

Rachel shrugged, "To be honest, I didn't know what to expect. I hoped you would be excited, but seeing as how none of us planned to be parents right now, well, I just didn't know."

"We're keeping it," Rogan snapped, looking disgusted that she would have even thought about an alternative.

"Fine, so we'll need to talk about the medical bills, because to be honest I'm not sure how I'll afford them, and what we're going to name the baby, and how we're going to work out visitation and custody."

The temperature in the room suddenly dropped twenty degrees and Rachel would have sworn she could see her own breath. All four men now looked at her with anger and frustration.

Rogan jumped in first with both feet. "Rachel, you don't need to concern yourself with the bills. We are more than well off, and we will handle the costs, whatever they may be. Custody is a moot point because you and the baby will be living here. As for the name—"

"What? Wait, no, you can't just decide that for me!"

Rogan shook his head and barreled on, "We'll need to get busy planning a wedding, and getting your place packed up."

"Wait a second, married? What are you talking about?" Rachel's head began to spin.

"But who is she going to marry, bro? I mean there are four of us, and she can only be legally married to one of us." Sawyer was speaking to Rogan, not to Rachel, and she began to feel like she was having an out of body experience. She could see herself standing in the middle of them gaping like a fish.

"It only makes sense she marry me because I'm the oldest. It doesn't really matter what the legal paperwork says, because she would be married in spirit to all of us. Right, love?"

The look on Rogan's face was one of determination, and her stomach rolled. She clenched her jaw together, slapping her hand over her mouth. She was stunned when Parker sprang out of his chair and bundled her up into his arms, before she could blink they were in the bathroom, and he was holding her hair as she emptied her stomach into the toilet. Not particularly graceful, but an unfortunately common occurrence for the last four weeks or so.

When she eased back onto her heels, feeling weak and trembly, Parker let go of her hair to get a glass of water and a washcloth. Tears were rolling down her cheeks as she sat on their bathroom floor feeling overwhelmed. How could she possibly explain to them that she needed more time to make decisions?

Hudson and Rogan were both happy about the news and wanted to marry her, but what did she actually feel? Sure, she was excited at the prospect of holding her and their child in her arms. But was she ready to commit to living and raising a child with them? Sawyer even seemed over the moon about it and it wasn't even his child. Weren't they even a little afraid, or disappointed that it happened this way? Maybe even angry that things weren't resolved first?

"It will all work out you know."

Parker. Her port in the storm. She could look to him to hold it together, and yet, when she looked up into his eyes all she saw was quiet ambivalence. Did he really feel the same way his brothers did, or did he think she got pregnant on purpose?

"Of course it will. Perhaps not like they hope, but it *will* all work out." She tried to sound confident, but her insides were still squirming and she knew if she tried to stand up right now her legs wouldn't hold her.

"How do you hope it will work out, Rachel? When you came here today, what was it you wanted from us?" Parker asked. He didn't move a muscle. He just sat there, staring at her in that deeply penetrating way that made her feel naked and vulnerable.

Rachel clenched her eyes shut, but tears stilled slipped from under her eyelids. What did she want exactly?

"I suppose I wanted acceptance, joy, support, I don't know," she whispered the words because they scared her.

Parker gave a small nod, and then sighed heavily. "Rachel, the day you left…we…well…let's just say it was rough. I apologize for pushing you so hard that morning, but I thought if we showed you how it could be with us…ah well hindsight is 20/20 right? I want to understand, Rachel, and I truly want to be happy for you and Rogan…or Hudson, but I have to know how you feel about this. Did you come back here to build a relationship, or just to pass along the news?"

"I just don't want to get hurt."

Parker's jaw ticked, and his nostrils flared, "Why are you so sure any of the four of us would hurt you?"

Shame flooded through her, but she didn't respond. What was she supposed to say? All men hurt their women at some point, so I may as well avoid men altogether. This whole situation was blowing up in her face because of her own issues, and she wasn't sure how to handle it from here on out.

"Can I have a minute to clean up in private."

For just a moment it looked like Parker was going to refuse, but he vanished out the bathroom door without another word, leaving her crying on the bathroom floor at her own selfish nature and ridiculous fears.

****

Nearly ten minutes passed before Rachel emerged from the bathroom with tear stained cheeks, and dull saddened eyes. Hudson held his hand out to her, but she pretended not to notice it as she took a seat in one of the single chairs, keeping some space between her and the four of them. It hurt that she was still scared of them, and Hudson was beginning to think things would never be okay again.

"I just want to say a couple of things," Rachel's voice was stronger than her eyes, and Hudson held his breath waiting for her to drop the hammer, "I have deep feelings for you guys, all four of you, but I'm not ready to get married and move in here. And just for the record that was the shittiest proposal I've ever heard of. Yes, I'm pregnant, but that doesn't mean I have to make rash decisions. If you four can forgive me for running away from you, I can promise you that I won't pull a stunt like that again without talking to you first. I don't know if this is forever, but…"

Hudson planned on Rachel being his wife, but she was right. She deserved more than an assumed marriage proposal. He wanted to give her wine and candlelight and rose petals when they asked her to marry them, but more importantly, he wanted to see love and not hesitation in her eyes when they did it.

"Forever is what we want with you, Rachel, but if you need a little more time we'll give it to you," Sawyer said, and Hudson nodded his agreement along with Parker and Rogan.

For the first time Rachel gave them an honest smile, and relief glowed from her eyes. "Thank you, that's all I can ask."

The group came back to life as Rogan grumbled to Parker about their marriage proposal being the shittiest versus practical, and Sawyer went to Rachel, pulling her up into his arms for a hug. His attempts to kiss her were thwarted and she groaned. "Not a chance! I just spent the last few minutes throwing up."

Sawyer looked disgruntled, and Hudson smacked his arm, "Bro, go get her a toothbrush from the medicine cabinet. She will kiss you when she's clean."

Rachel giggled as Sawyer headed off in search of the requested toothbrush, and Hudson took her hand. "Are you having a lot of morning sickness, honey?"

"Some, but it's not always in the mornings. I seem to get sick to my stomach every time I get emotional, and every time I smell eggs," she answered, letting him pull her against his chest. He buried his nose into her hair, deeply inhaling the sweet scent that was all her own, and sighed with pleasure when she wrapped her arms around his waist and hugged him back.

"I guess that means I'm not cooking breakfast for you in the morning," Sawyer said, coming back in and handing her a brand new toothbrush.

"I can't stay the night tonight, guys. I have a meeting tomorrow morning at eight with the Rafts. Randal finally signed the paperwork with me to sell their place, and I need to go over and work out an open house schedule."

Hudson nodded, and kissed her forehead. "That's okay, honey, we understand. But we would like you to spend more time out here at the ranch. Hopefully someday you'll feel like this is your home too. Now, when did you say that first doctor's appointment was?"

Chapter Fifteen

Rachel sat in Diana Raft's kitchen the next morning holding a cup of coffee in her hands while Randal and Diana looked over the paperwork for their listing. The ranch was large, and it was a prime piece of grazing land, but the house and barn needed a lot of work. By the disappointed look on Randal's face, Rachel knew he was expecting to list the place for more money than it was worth.

"Are you sure that's the right figure?" he asked her, squinting at the numbers.

She nodded, "Yeah. I'm sorry, Randal, but you know that home values are down. We can list it for a higher number, but I'm afraid it will just sit here for months. I know how much you guys want to get moved to be closer to your daughter." She let her voice drift off, not wanting to point out the abbreviated amount of the time that Diana had left in this world.

"I just hate to see it get undervalued. If I'm going to sell it, then I want to get what it's really worth," he argued, dropping the paper to pinch the bridge of his nose.

"Randy, we've lived here for almost forty years. Forty great years, but the value you think it has is sentimental. It's time to let another family build their memories on this land." Diana was the voice of reason in this relationship, and Rachel watched in awe as the woman talked her husband down. "Besides, you and I both know this house isn't worth anything. It's the land that has value. There are several prosperous ranches around us that would be glad to take it off our hands. I want to go see Breanna, darling. You said yourself it's important the next few months be spent with our family."

Randal reached out to take Diana's hand in his own and he brought it to his lips in a gesture that reminded Rachel of her own four men. When the older gentleman finally turned his attention back to Rachel, he had tears in his eyes.

"Done. Nothing is more important than my woman. Is there anything else I need to sign?"

"No, Randal, you've signed it all. I just wanted to make sure we were all on the same page before the listing goes up Monday morning. I'll want to have an open house next weekend if that's alright with you both."

Diana and Randal both nodded. "I'll start packing some stuff up to ship to Bre this week, and Randy can make sure the barn is cleaned up."

"Now don't go wearing yourself out, Diana-doll. We can hire someone in here to do the packing." Randal flashed a smile at Rachel, "Silly woman still thinks she can do everything herself."

"Oh I can still manage my own packing. Now that I'm not doing the treatments anymore I have a little more strength." Diana directed the last statement to Rachel who nodded politely.

"Well, I better get back to work. Tanner Kegan is coming by later to look at the last of the herd. I think he's going to buy the tractor too. No sense keeping it when we won't be tilling up the land." Randal kissed his wife and then waved goodbye to Rachel before hurrying out of the house.

After a pause the back screen door slammed shut behind him, and Diana let out her breath in a whoosh. She gave Rachel a half smile, "I'm sorry, he's struggling with all of this. It's been so hard on him."

"It's okay, Diana. I do understand. I can't even imagine how hard it is for both of you." Rachel tried not to let the pity she was feeling show. Diana was such a strong woman, even sitting across from her with her hair in thin patchy clumps, and her arms bruised and pocked from IV pokes. She looked proud and determined to defeat the demons invading her world. Only, Rachel knew this demon was undefeatable. Cancer was going to be the thing to bring Diana down.

"I have loved that man for more than four decades. We raised two children together, buried one of them, watched the other get married and move across the country, and now we're at the end, just trying to hold on for one more precious minute." Diana played with the gold band that hung loosely on the ring finger of her left hand, spinning it around and around her thin finger.

Rachel's heart lurched in her chest at the love and pain that radiated from the woman. "I admire you so much, Diana. I hope someday I can have a love like yours and Randal's."

That seemed to perk Diana up, and she narrowed her eyes on Rachel. "I've heard the rumors, Rach. There is something between you and those Brooks boys."

A blush of embarrassment warmed Rachel's cheeks, but she didn't deny it. What was the point? She was having a baby with one of them, and the whole town would know it soon enough. "I care about them."

Diana watched her with her head tipped and her hand holding her chin thoughtfully. "You know, the day I agreed to marry Randal was the same day I broke off my engagement to another man. I actually left him standing at the church in his suit and tie waiting to say the 'I do's'. I had been seeing Randal behind Gary's back, and most of the town knew it. I wasn't brave enough to admit my feelings to either of them, until it was almost too late."

Rachel listened in silent surprise. Diana was a pillar of the community, so it was odd to think she might have been the source of scandal at any point in her life.

"The only other time I've done something so stupid, was when I found out I was sick and didn't tell Randal right away. I thought I was protecting him, but ultimately I was denying him some of the precious time he needed to deal with his own feelings and grieve for me." Diana stared past Rachel's head as she spoke, lost in her own world of pain. "If you care for them, Rachel, do yourself and them the courtesy of being honest about it. Don't let time slip away from you, because one day you look around, and it's all over. You can't back up and start again, or change the course…you just have to live it out and let it happen."

Tears spilled out of Rachel's eyes and down her cheeks. Her pregnancy emotions seemed to be more and more chaotic, and Diana was hitting a nerve. "I'm in love with them."

Diana smiled softly, "All four of them, right?" At Rachel's nod, Diana let out a small laugh, "I suspected as much. Those four do everything together, so it only made sense they would want to share the same woman. So what's the problem? Why are you telling me and not them?"

"You know about my dad." Rachel grimaced when Diana nodded. "He has another family now, a couple of a kids and a happy life, but he hasn't spoken to me in years. My mom and him seemed so happy right up until he just all of a sudden fell out of love with her. How does that happen? How do you go from loving something enough to pledge the rest of your life to them, and then suddenly one day, you just don't anymore?"

"It's different for everyone, Rachel, but you were young when that all happened. It's possible you don't know the whole story between your parents. Have you ever asked them?"

Rachel frowned, "I know enough. And besides, it's not just my dad. Every man I've ever trusted has cheated on me or betrayed my trust. Mitch was just the most recent mistake I've made, but he sure wasn't the first. I can't let myself keep getting hurt."

Diana gave her a disapproving frown. "I probably should keep my mouth shut but, Rachel, you're being silly. Can't you see that it's not all men, it's just the men you've picked? Your picker is off, girl! Now, from what I hear, the Brooks boys seduced you, which means you didn't do the picking. I would say that means there is a better chance of this being a good relationship. Do you trust them?"

"Yes," Rachel said without any hesitation.

"Then go to them. Tell them. Don't wait until it's too late to realize what love is. Love is trusting the other person enough to put your heart in their hands, but it's also coming to the understanding that *you* hold *their* heart in your hands, and can do them irreparable damage."

Rachel sat silently mulling over Diana's words, and staring into her cup of coffee like it was a magic eight ball and she was waiting for the right answer. Diana seemed to sense that she had said enough, because she stood and carried her own mug to the sink.

"And, Rachel," when Rachel finally looked up the woman smiled, "coffee isn't good for the baby. You should cut your caffeine intake."

Rachel felt her face drain of blood as she stared into the other woman's cloudy blue eyes. "What?"

"Oh, did you think I couldn't tell? Sweetie, I've had two babies of my own, and you're moping around like a hurt mama bear. How far along are you?"

"Eight weeks," Rachel whispered.

Diana's smile was wide, and she nodded. "Well, I won't make it to see your little one, but I hope that you and its fathers will be very happy together for as many years as Randy and I have been."

"Thank you, Diana. You've been…well…you've given me some food for thought."

"You're welcome, Rachel. We'll see you next weekend."

With that, Rachel gathered her things, and made a beeline for Brooks Pastures. She had just realized that she had a few more things to say to her men.

****

Rachel arrived at the ranch to find a strange man she hadn't met in the barn. The excitement burning in her chest eased a little as she frowned at the stranger. He was big. Bigger than any of the four Brooks brothers—and that was saying a lot. Rachel nearly swallowed her tongue as she took in the wide shoulders that looked like they wouldn't even fit through a doorway. Blonde curls peeked out from under a worn red bandana that was damp with sweat, and his body was hunched over as he worked silently.

"Hello?"

The man looked up from the saddle he was working on and she got a glimpse of gorgeous blue eyes and a pair of matching dimples as he grinned, "Hi! You must be Rachel. The boys were telling me about you. I'm Mack Thompson. You've got them all tied up in knots, little lady."

Rachel liked him immediately, and moved closer to watch him as he tooled the leather. "They have been pretty crazy too, that's beautiful. Did you do all of that?"

Mack nodded, "Yeah, it's kind of a hobby."

"So, I haven't seen you in town, Mack, how long have you been in Stone River?"

"I met Parker at the club a couple of years back, and after my leather business went belly up last summer he offered me a job on the ranch. I've only been her a few months, and I'm not much for socializing. I stay around here most of the time."

Rachel frowned, "What club?"

The blush of embarrassment that stole up Mack's cheeks caught her off guard, and he glanced away. "Um, well, uh…that would be The Cage. It's a BDSM club."

"Oh….*oh!*" Now Rachel felt a little embarrassed herself. There was an awkward pause before she changed the subject. "Do you know where the guys are?"

"Yeah, they are out on the West line, by the pond. There was some fencing that got damaged when a tree fell over in the storm last week."

Rachel nodded, and then frowned. "Do you think I can borrow a horse? I really need to talk to them."

Mack's eyes squinted just a minute as he evaluated her question before he agreed. "Done, but if they ask how you did it, leave my name out of it. The rules I got were to keep you safe when you were around, and I doubt they meant letting you ride off alone."

Rachel rolled her eyes, "It will be our little secret, Mack. I promise!"

Chapter Sixteen

Rachel rode carefully but quickly as she made her way across the ranch. She was no expert and her nerves were fluttering the whole time, but in less than an hour she had located her men. Her mouth watered when she spotted them working on the fence line. Parker and Sawyer were both shirtless, and their golden tan colored skin glowed in the sunlight. It was Hudson who spotted her first and gestured her way.

They all four froze and waited as she drew closer. About forty feet out, Parker cursed and moved to meet her in the middle. She was giggling when he tugged her down off the horse.

"Just what do you think you're doing, Rachel? Riding a horse when you're pregnant? And doing it alone! My God, you could have fallen, or gotten lost, or—"

"I love you, too, Parker Brooks," she interrupted him, and then laughed when his mouth fell open.

"What?"

"You heard me. I love you. I know you're worried about me, because you're protective of me, and I love that part of you. I love every part of you, and I love your brothers." Rachel turned as the other three men drew into a tight circle around her. Rogan stood at her back, as he always would, holding her and supporting her as the rock of their family. Sawyer stood to her right, bringing her fingers to his lips to kiss their tips. She loved the crooked smile on his face as his eyes flashed with heated amusement. Hudson was on her left, his fingers laced tightly through hers, and their clasped hands clutched against his heart. Emotions rolled through his dark eyes, but the strongest one was love. She could see it now, and instead of scaring her, it made her horny as fuck. Turning back to face Parker, she looked up into his eyes. He stood toe to toe with her, and all she wanted to do was let him hold her. He had asked her to trust him, and to submit to him, and now she really understood what that meant.

"I want you four to be in my life, and our child's life, forever. I'm not perfect, and you guys haven't even seen me at my worst. Just wait until PMS returns in full force, but if you still want me, I'm yours. I want you, Sir." When she finished talking, she let her eyes drop to the center of his glorious chest while she waited for his response. It was more than she could have hoped for, as he jerked her against his chest, pulling her away from his brothers and kissing her for all she was worth.

He seemed to pour his emotions into her mouth, his soul expanding and locking with hers on their shared breath. It was monumental, and she melted under the pressure, letting it consume her and light her on fire.

When they broke apart, he gripped her hair and roughly pulled her head back so she would look at him. "I don't know what changed, and I'm not sure I care. I love you too, sunshine. With every part of me, I love you. Are you sure you can handle all of me?"

She grinned and lifted one eyebrow, "Give it your worst, cowboy."

There was a loud whoop from behind her, and she was again wrapped in between four sweaty sexy cowboys. She felt hands moving over every part of her body, more hands than her chaotic brain could follow as they stripped her of her clothes, baring her skin to the warm sunshine. This was the culmination of the neurotic and emotionally charged journey she had been on for the last two months, and it was magnificent. Parker wasted no time in taking the lead and directed Sawyer to retrieve a saddle blanket, which was spread in the grass while Rogan and Parker entertained her mouth and hands.

Rachel didn't even see them strip their clothes off, but suddenly Sawyer was at her side thrusting his hard cock into her tight fist. She gave him a squeeze and began a gentle stroking motion. Rogan seemed to appreciate Sawyer's creativity because her other palm was filled with his dick next, and she let her head tip back onto Parker's chest as he fingered her cunt. Hudson was suckling her nipples and biting at her belly button ring. The constant touches were making her delirious, and she felt her knees begin to shake.

"Guys, I'm going to fall!" she whimpered, trying to point out her weakness. Parker's arm went around her waist and he clutched her tightly to him.

"Never, Rachel. You will never fall because we'll always catch you," his words were soft, but they were potent, and she shattered in an intense orgasm. Her hands must have squeezed just a bit too tightly due to her climax, because Sawyer yelped and tugged her fist away from him.

"Easy now, baby, you pull that off and we're both going to be upset." She laughed at him until he claimed her mouth, and distracted her from what his brothers were doing.

The rough sensation of saddle rope scraped across her arm and she jumped when Rogan and Parker gripped her hands pulling them together. Parker was quick to lace the rope around her wrists and she stood in stunned silence. He wanted to tie her up out here in front of his brothers, seriously? Her eyes darted up to take in his small smirk of satisfaction as he tested the knotted ropes.

"Do you remember your safe words?"

She shivered as his sexy voice filled her ears, and gave a small nod. "Yes, Sir."

"Good, because, sunshine, I'm keeping you tied up this time so you can't run off when we're done. In fact, I may never remove the ropes again."

Her eyes widened until he laughed, "Uh, I doubt you're going to want me tied up when the baby arrives. That would leave you four in charge of a newborn."

Sawyer's face looked a little pale and he grimaced. "The ropes will come off soon enough, baby, just let him have his moment."

"What's with all of the talking? We have a naked woman here who just agreed to be our wife, let's get on with it!" Rogan grabbed the knotted rope and tugged her off balance so she fell against his chest with a giggle. His mouth came down on hers, reminding her of the love and passion that filled his soul for her. He took her breath away, and she felt tears stinging her eyelids when he drew away.

Before she could get her bearings back, she was settled over the top of Hudson who was waiting on his back on the blanket fisting his own erection. She sank down over it with a heavy sigh of pleasure. Just having that physical connection with one of her men settled her whole world back on its axis again.

It dawned on her a moment later that he wasn't wearing a condom when she spotted Sawyer coating his cock in lube.

"Do you always carry lube with you, cowboy?" she taunted as Hudson gripped her hips and pushed her to rock with him.

Sawyer flashed her a wicked grin and shook his head. "Nah, this isn't even mine. Rogan had it in his saddlebag. Something about a cowgirl taking him for a ride this one time."

Rachel giggled until Hudson pushed her backwards, angling her body so the head of his dick rubbed against her G-spot.

Parker knelt to the side, gripping her tied wrists in his hand behind her back while his mouth dropped to her breasts. With the angle that she was, draped over Hudson, her tits were lifted high into the air. Between the two of them she was swiftly losing the ability to think.

Sawyer moved to stand just behind her, but the way she was positioned, her head rested level with his thighs. He fisted his lube-coated cock in his hand, but his balls swung free and heavy, so she took advantage of the position to lick the seam that split them.

"Fuck!" Hearing his reaction, she nearly climaxed again.

"Rachel, you did not have permission to touch Sawyer yet. That's ten, sunshine," Parker said just before he bit down on her nipple. She shrieked and struggled to sit up for a moment before realizing she didn't have enough leverage, and the muscles in her back were weakening from the odd angle.

Forcing herself to relax she looked up at Sawyer from under her lashes, "I'm so sorry, Sir. Please forgive me."

Sawyer's eyes blazed with fire, and he dropped to his knees between Hudson's spread feet to kiss her. He pushed her back up to a sitting position on Hudson. "No calling me 'Sir', baby. I'm Sawyer, or if you really want to give me a pet name I could live with His Majesty."

She was laughing again when Sawyer pushed her down over Hudson's chest and settled in behind her. He began rubbing the fat head of his cock against her anus, easing inside just a half an inch or so, and then pulling back, until the muscles relaxed and let him sink into her. He held her by one hip and her bound wrists, and began to guide the movement between the three of them. Hudson would push in, when Sawyer pulled out, and then they would reverse.

Rachel clenched her eyes shut, and let her body relax into their direction. When a rough hand tangled in her hair, she let out a gasp of desire and her mouth dropped open. The thick cock that pushed inside belonged to Parker, and she instinctively swallowed against the intrusion. Determined to get what he wanted, Parker surged back into her mouth and out almost simultaneously with Hudson's thrusts into her pussy.

Groaning loudly, Sawyer climaxed deep inside of her, and Parker quickly followed. She swallowed every drop of cum, enjoying the little bit of control she had as he shuddered with each tease of her tongue. Rogan moved in behind her and took Sawyer's place, again filling her completely, and finishing the circle when he and Hudson proceeded to fuck her mindless.

She was lost to them, decadently submitting to the four men that she planned to spend the rest of her life with. It was sinful, and sweet. By the time they had all four been sated her body was a delicious pile of boneless goo, and she sported the most erotic pair of rope burns around her wrists.

"So, baby, what happened? Yesterday you seemed so determined to keep your distance."

Sawyer was behind her so she couldn't see him when he asked, but she knew this was too important not to do it face to face. She had to twist out of Rogan's grip so she could sit up in order to make eye contact with all of them. Sitting there on the saddle blanket under the afternoon sun, with four gloriously nude Brooks brothers, was like a scene out of a romance novel. They were all four completely focused on her and what she was going to say.

"I had my meeting with Diana and Randall Raft, and she gave me a few words of wisdom. I don't know if this is going to last forever. I just know that I want to enjoy being happy with the four of you right now. Gossip be damned." She could feel her chin set with determination, and as she looked around there was a myriad of emotions on the four masculine faces.

Parker's satisfied smirk was tempered with the glint of pride, while Rogan and Sawyer looked relieved. Hudson looked smug, and she narrowed her gaze on him. "What is that look for, Mr. Brooks?"

"Oh nothing, honey. I was just planning the rest of our lives, that's all." He laughed when she pinched his bare thigh, and reached for her, tugging her down on top of him. "Okay, so I suppose we had better plan the wedding first, huh?"

"You better believe it, Mister! I want the dress, the flowers, the minister, and all four of my men in tuxes."

Four matching groans sent her into a riot of giggles as they tried to convince her to forgo the tuxedoes. It was Rogan who sealed the deal when he took her chin in his hand and grabbed her attention.

"I will wear whatever you want, as long as you say "I do, forever."

Her heart melted and she felt the love spill over until tears were slipping down her cheeks. "I love you, Rogan."

"I love you, too, sexy."

"Hey, I love you, too, baby!" Sawyer kissed her shoulder, while Hudson rubbed her feet.

"Well, I loved her first," Parker argued with a slap on her naked ass. "And I intend on loving her again and again and again…"

That set off another round of lovemaking as the afternoon shifted to evening and the fence was forgotten for the day. Never before had Rachel felt so loved. Wrapped up in the middle of a tangle of legs and sweat covered masculine bodies, she knew there would never be a better place for her, and she sent up her thanks to whatever twist of fate brought five star crossed lovers together into this one place and time.

Epilogue

"Dude, I can't do this." Sawyer looked terrified, and Parker frowned at him.

"What do you mean you can't do this? There is no backing out, man. It's happening, one way or another." Parker crossed his arms over his chest and glared at his younger brother.

"But, Parker, this just isn't right. I think I need more time." Sawyer glanced away guiltily and Parker had to clench his hands into fists to keep from punching him.

"Sawyer Brooks, if you don't take your turn changing our daughter's diaper, I will personally beat you until you scream for mercy."

Sawyer looked a little green at the gills, but Parker refused to back down. He glanced down at the tiny bundle of pink laying on the changing table between the two of them and smiled. Juliet Diana Brooks was the picture of perfection with her mother's heart shaped face, and her father's dark eyes. A perfect eight pounds four ounces of sweet baby girl, and Parker was as in love with her as he was with her mother.

The last eight months had passed in a blur of wedding plans, moving Rachel in, purchasing the Raft place, and piles of baby supplies, all culminating in the birth of the beautiful Juliet. They hadn't had a DNA test done, because they all decided they didn't really care who her biological father was. She carried the Brooks name, and she would forever have four fathers who doted on her.

Now, if Parker could just get Sawyer to step it up in the diaper changing department.

"I mean it, Sawyer. You've been avoiding this for the last six weeks. You can't spend the first two years of her life avoiding her because you don't want to change her diaper."

"I'm not avoiding her! I feed her and rock her, and snuggle her all the time." Sawyer looked affronted, and Parker rolled his eyes.

"Yeah, but the moment it's time for a diaper change you suddenly disappear. This one is all you buddy. Get to it." Parker held up a diaper that was smaller than his own hand, and Sawyer reached for it. There was a slight tremble to his fingers as he took it, and Parker huffed.

"She doesn't bite, Sawyer."

"What if she pees on me?"

"Then you will just have to change her clothes. Come on, lil' bro, we've all done this a hundred times already. You're the only chicken left," Rogan said, stepping into the room with a bottle in his hand. "Besides, Jules needs changed before she can have her lunch and take her nap. Her mommy just got home from the doctor with the all clear, but she isn't letting anyone seduce her until she is assured that her precious princess is sleeping peacefully. So hurry the fuck up."

That got a reaction. Sawyer took a deep breath and began to carefully remove the diaper from Juliet's tiny body. By the time he had wrapped the tape around her tiny waist and re-buttoned her onesie, sweat had broken out on his brow.

Parker laughed as Sawyer scooped up his daughter and clutched her to his chest with a sigh of relief. "Okay, that wasn't so bad."

"Yeah, just wait until you do the next poopy one," Rogan said with a laugh as he passed the bottle to a horrified Sawyer.

This was their new world. It consisted of babies, and diapers, and naps and a happiness that Parker Brooks never imagined he would find. He had the best wife in the world, even if she was more of a brat than a submissive.

His thoughts of her seemed to draw her out, and he felt her step up behind him. "Hey, cowboy."

"Hey yourself, sunshine. I hear you had a good checkup."

She moved around to face him, pressing her full breasts against his chest, and grinned. "Yep, the doctor gave me the all clear to resume all activities."

"Perfect. I have some rope that I've been wanting to try out," he murmured, brushing a kiss over her full lips.

Her shiver of anticipation and dilated pupils gave away her desire, and his cock throbbed in his jeans. "Mmm…I suppose I better find a crop."

He recoiled in surprise, "What?"

Her laughter followed her as she moved down the hallway. "It's been six weeks, cowboy. You're going to need more than just a rope, because it's going to be a wild ride."

THE END

Books by Lori King

Published by JK Publishing, Inc.:

The Surrender Trilogy

Weekend Surrender
Book One

Coming Soon: Book Two

Published by Siren-Bookstrand:

The Gray Pack Series

Fire of the Wolf
Reflections of the Wolf
Legacy of the Wolf
Dreams of the Wolf

Apache Crossing Series

Sidney's Triple Shot

Sunset Point Series

Point of Seduction

I would love to hear from you!

Website: www.lorikingbooks.wordpress.com
Facebook: www.facebook.com/lori.king.author

Email: lorikingbooks@yahoo.com

JK Publishing, Inc.

Excerpt from Rush Against Time
Twisted Fates Series Book One
by Willow Brooke

Jessa Meadows shifted her weight between each foot unable to stand still. Today had proven to be even worse than the previous with no end in sight. The past few months had been a hurricane of agonizing disastrous events. With a huff, she slung her silky golden hair over her shoulder and handed the huge cup of coffee across the counter to the disgruntled and obviously caffeine deprived woman. When she turned around to grab the glass blender pitcher, she knocked it off onto the tile floor and it exploded into shards.

Jessa cursed under her breath at the broken glass that lay scattered around her feet. The past six months she had been slammed straight into her first heat with a vengeance. The more she fought it, the longer it dragged on and the more intense it grew. What was supposed to be a milestone in growing up as a shifter had become a living nightmare. It was similar to human puberty, only jacked up on steroids. A shifter could not scent their mate or be scented by their mate until after losing their virginity, or receiving a kiss from them. It was expected of all shifters to experiment sexually during this time, where in the human world it was socially and morally wrong to scratch every hormonal itch. Like wild animals, they would bang every single wolf who so much as gave them a wink and a smile. It was an animalistic fuck fest, and Jessa wanted no part of it. Her wolf fought for control, lunging at every weak spot in an attempt to take over. She was mentally drained, and physically restless. Obviously clumsy could be added to the growing list now, too. *Yippie freakin' skippy.* Frustration pooled in the rims of her eyes and threatened to spill as she cleaned up the shards.

Every man within sniffing distance was all up in her personal space, eagerly offering his services in every humorous and pathetic way possible. The problem was, she refused to give her virginity to the first mutt that came along. It might be unheard of in shifter society, but Jessa wanted her first time to be meaningful. The idea of falling on her back for the first horn dog that came along at the right time made her stomach turn.

Lost deep in the recess of her thoughts while robotically preparing the next order at Mocha Express, her wolf growled and pranced in a challenging dance at the scents that wafted in her direction. The sudden yelp from the group of girls at the counter was a reality mental slap. The animalistic noise must have slipped out, because they now looked at her as if she had grown a tail. She had to resist the urge to peek behind her and make sure she hadn't. *Super.* Jessa offered up a sweet smile, hoping it would dissipate their sudden shock. Mocha Express was one of the few chains that catered to both humans and otherworldly creatures, offering treats and beverages for shifters, vampires, and many other magical creatures that humans were oblivious to. Plus, it provided cover for the group that occupied the attached mansion.

Vampires and shifters took up residency at Gates Manor, a huge mansion that dated back into the eighteenth century. The eclectic group of paranormal prodigies worked together to keep the balance of the world in order. To prevent the devil from spreading evil through demon possessions and taking over the magical community, angels banded together with this elite group and gave direct orders for them to follow. Not many knew of the group's existence, and great measures were taken to keep it that way. They were known as the Guardians by the select few who helped and fought with them on each mission.

Michael Stone was the head vampire in the agency, who was in charge of all of the vampires on the continent. He had a huge army of vampires at his ready who fought without question and at a moment's notice. His wife, Christina, was *the* most powerful witch who originated from the first bloodline. Her aunt Autumn had been until Christina accepted her powers in the moon ritual. Together, the duo was unbeatable. Most witches needed three to harness magic to their full abilities. Autumn and Christina didn't.

Next was Alan Black, one of Autumn's two mates. He was the alpha of the wolf shifters in Northern America and represented them in the Guardians. Her other mate, Braden Wilder, was the alpha of the jaguar shifters in North America and also member of the Guardians. Together, they all made up one big, happy—odd family.

Working the day shift at Mocha Express meant more humans and the need to contain her wolf better, but it also meant less shifters that her mangy mutt would try to jump on. It was a catch-22.

Unfortunately, word must have gotten out of her schedule change. The door chimed announcing the arrival of the mob of six shifter men, all sporting huge grins and hungry looks. The intensity shooting from their eyes confirmed the hunger they had wouldn't be sated with Danish rolls or pastries. Anger immediately boiled through her veins. *Tough luck, boys. You aren't getting your hands on my cookies. Make a move. I dare you.*

Quickly drawing her attention back to the task-at-hand, she hurriedly finished the order and braced herself for the scene that was about to unfold. With her wolf chomping at the bit, she gritted her teeth and shoved the animal back into its restraints. *Time for some fun. Let's see if you boys can keep up!* She plastered the biggest smile she could muster, and turned to her overeager customers. "Good afternoon, gentlemen! What can I get for you today?"

Mated
by Avery Gale
Coming October 1st from JK Publishing, Inc.

    Jameson Wolf had been almost ready to head home when he'd taken one last look out of the front windows of his office. Looking down over the sidewalk below, he wondered why the waiting line was so long on a frigid Friday night. He'd started to turn back to the room when his eye caught on a flash of red. Damn it to hell, he'd always had a thing for auburn haired women. Redheads were rare among shifters so he took a closer look. It might have been her long flowing mane of red curls that caught his attention, but there was something about her saucy attitude that drew him in. Watching her, he saw her easy rapport with the tiny blonde beauty she was with and he liked the fact that she seemed oblivious to the fact that she turned the head of every man near her.
    Making his way down the steep circular staircase he was assailed by the overpowering scents of both humans and his peers who had braved the biting cold January night in the wind swept city. He saw the red-haired beauty enter through the heavy doorway a split second before the scent of his mate barreled over him. It was as if every neuron in his brain had been suddenly struck by lightning and was now crackling with electrical energy. His vision tunneled and his sole mission became to find the owner of that scent and mark her as his.
    As he neared the red-haired beauty who had caught his eye earlier, the exotic fragrance he'd been following became more and more potent. *Could I actually be that lucky after all these years?* Stepping up behind her he took a deep breath letting her scent soak deeply into his soul. Even though he loved the fresh citrus smell of her hair, it was the essence of her that was nearly over-powering in its allure. It pulled him in and made every one of his senses come sharply into a

pinpoint focus. He'd heard his friends describe this moment, but he had truly believed that their words had been little more than romantic folly—until now.

When she turned toward him, he became instantly aware that she'd been planning to escape. There was a look of panic in her eyes—what he didn't understand was what had spooked her. Awareness and anxiety were coming off her in heavy, crashing waves. He could smell fear in humans and shifters, but that wasn't what he was picking up. No, she wasn't afraid of him, but she wasn't thrilled to have been found either. *Interesting.* Mating scents are an almost overwhelmingly powerful draw for both male and female shifters so there was no doubt she had known her mate was near. So why was she trying to leave?

Both Jameson and his brother, Trevlon, were the Alphas of their pack and had been since their fathers were killed by rivals seven years ago. They had always known they'd follow pack tradition and share a mate, but they hadn't had any luck finding her despite having traveled all over the globe searching. *How has this beauty flown under our radar? She is exactly the type of woman we are both attracted to.* "What is your name, beautiful?" Jameson knew his words had come out as more of a growl than a question, but considering how close he was to claiming her right here in the middle of the club, it was the best he could do. He relaxed a bit when he saw her deer in the headlights look. *Good – I'm happy to know she is as slammed by the attraction as I am.*

"Kit." He heard the wobble of nervousness in her voice and could tell she had barely been able to squeak out the word so he just waited. He saw her draw in a deep breath through her mouth and almost laughed at her ineffective attempt to avoid breathing through her nose. He tried to suppress his smile when she repeated the gesture because it was a futile attempt to escape the scent of her mate.

Once a shifter found their mate, their bodies were taken over by overwhelming sexual urges that lasted for weeks. He'd seen pack members all but disappear during that time because they could barely leave their bedrooms. He waited patiently as she finally seemed to come back to awareness and answered, "I mean, Kathleen, my name is Kathleen Harris." She was trying to look around him, which was amusing because she couldn't be more than five feet three or four inches tall and that was including the ridiculously high-heeled black leather stiletto boots she was wearing.

He was sure she hadn't meant to give him her nickname because it was likely something she reserved for those she considered close friends, so when he addressed her again, he used it deliberately. "Well, Kit, follow me, please."

He turned on his heel and started back toward the staircase when she reached out and grasped his forearm. "Wait, I can't go with you. I don't even know you. And my friend will be looking for me." The instant she touched him he'd felt a jolt of electricity arc between them and then tiny bolts of lightning streaked up his spine. *Damn, her touch did that through the fabric of his shirt, what would it feel like when they were skin to skin?*

The twin bond between him and Trev had always been incredibly strong, so he wasn't at all surprised when his phone rang. "Where are you? Are you okay?" Typical Trevlon, straight to it—he couldn't be troubled to utter a polite greeting.

"Standing in front of a woman I want you to meet. We're in the bar, but we'll be on our way upstairs as soon as we locate her friend to let her know where we are heading. Meet us in the office in five." Jameson disconnected the call and turned to one of his staff that was walking by. He quickly gave the man a detailed description of Kit's friend and instructions to stay close to her and keep her safe until she was ready to leave the building. At that time, he was to accompany her to the office. Jameson stood six foot seven inches tall in his boots, so he could easily see the tiny blonde on the other side dance floor and directed the young man to her. Jameson was glad it had been Charlie who'd been the first to walk by. He trusted the young shifter to do exactly as he'd been told.

Turning back to Kit, he realized for the first time that he had taken the hand she'd used to grab his arm and was holding it in his own. He'd been rubbing small circles over the inside of her wrist with his thumb. As his gaze met hers he felt her pulse speed up and watched as her pupils dilated. "Come along, Kit. We need to talk." This time he did smell fear so he pulled her into his arms and leaned down so his words would be painted over the soft shell of her ear like a warm brush of air, "I won't hurt you—ever. Be brave, sweet kitten."

Rane's Giant
by Lynn Ray Lewis
Coming October 8th from JK Publishing, Inc.

As soon as Lord Ludwig left she crawled from behind the big chest, and slowly approached the prisoner. He had not moved since they brought him in and shackled him to the wall. Her hands began to warm as she slowly ran them from the top of his head to the tips of his toes so she could assess the damage done to his body.

This man had taken a beating like none before him. His skull was a web of cracked bone, and three of his ribs were completely broken, with one sticking out from his flesh. His thickly muscled legs were striped by fresh rope marks, and his entire body was bruised with deep painful injuries. The stab wound in his gut worried her a bit, but not as much as the cracked skull.

This warrior had not gone down easily.

She had to sit astraddle his thick muscular thighs to reach his head with her hands. *Goddess, but the man was huge.* Her legs were spread so far apart she could feel the burning stretch in her own thighs. It was good he was unconscious because she could feel the thick bulge of his man's organ nestled between her own sex.

Rane placed her hands on his head over the worst of the webbed bones under his hair and skin. She began the tedious task of melding the bone back together, making sure to interlock every small shard of bone so none would be left to float around in his skull after she healed him. Any tiny sliver of bone could cause damage and pain later, so it was better to get the pesky things taken care of the first time and be done with it.

She leaned over him for hours, concentrating on healing his skull, and pushing the gel that was causing pressure on his brain to seep out of the lesser openings where the skin was broken. Even if she had water to wash away the blood, she would not have done it yet. It would take another day, at least, to heal the rest of his injuries enough to remove him from this place, and place a pile of ashes in his spot.

Rane was getting quite a collection of big men hiding in the cave near the river. As soon as she heard that the Lord had a new prisoner, she slipped into the dungeon through the secret rock in the wall, and observed the guards and the Lord or Simon come into the room to torture the men for information.

When they left the men beaten and shackled at death's door, she slipped through the wall and healed them enough to secrete them out of the room, and into the small tunnel leading into the forest.

Today's discovery of a new prisoner was merely happenstance. She had been hiding in the dungeon because this was the one place Simon rarely ventured into without his small gang of hangers-on. She again thanked the Goddess for the small size of her body as she hid behind the trunk of torture implements in the darkest corner. There had been no time to hide in the tunnel without being seen by the guards.

That she was already here in this room when they brought him in was a blessing for the warrior had he but known it. The bleeding in his brain causing the swelling would have killed him after days of torturous pain. That is, if the stab wounds and the blood seeping from the place his rib stuck through his flesh had not caused him to bleed to death. Or the wound became infected with filth, and he died from the infection.

Rane took her hands from the warriors head and waited for the wounds to bleed a little more before sealing the seeping wounds on the inside of his flesh. That way, when his captors came back they would see what it appeared to be. The huge man still incapacitated from his mortal wounds, complete with fresh blood still slowly causing him to bleed to death. They liked that. They took bets on how long a prisoner would still bleed, and even how much they would bleed before death. Almost to a man, Lord Ludwig's men were as depraved as he and his sibling.

It puzzled her as to why this warrior, and the past three like him, had not been killed outright on the battlefield as so many had been. Nor had they been subjected to the lord's usual depravities. For some reason he seemed to fear these men, and when a small pile of ashes had been found where the prisoner had been chained, all he did was grunt and nod his head. He ordered his guards to sweep up every ash, and scatter the ashes into the wind over the fields.

When the lord felt particularly like he needed entertainment, and there were no prisoners in the dungeon, he would have a villager brought into the hall on a trumped up charge, and allow his men to torture the poor soul. The villagers were raped and beaten for screaming during the process. One man had been strung up over the blackened beams overhead, and roasted over a vat of bubbling fat. His screams were said to still echo in the hall on cold nights.

Sadly, by the time each villager was tossed out of the hall like a pile of garbage, if still alive, their mind was too broken for Rane to heal them. She might heal their bodies, but the mind was in the hands of the Goddess.